"You are a miserable excuse for a person if you don't buy this hilarious book. Bob Powers is some kind of comedy genius or something. Frankly, I'm scared."

> —Paul Feig, creator of the TV series *Freaks and Geeks* and author of *Superstud*

"There are page-turners and then there are page-turners. This wonderful, pathetic tale left me wanting more pages."

> —Zach Galifianakis, humorist

"No one I know writes so funny and so sad at the same time better than Bob Powers. If you're willing to take a chance and jump into his twisted mind, you're in for a delicious, cringe-inducing treat. . . . This book is like those great Choose Your Own Adventure books we read as kids, if the pain and soul-crushing responsibility of adulthood had infested the whole thing."

> —Bryan Tucker, writer for *Chappelle's Show* and *Saturday Night Live*

"As I read Bob Powers's Just Make a Choice! adventure, I endeavored to choose honestly, according to my own ethics and beliefs. Unfortunately, this resulted in babies being aborted, people being murdered, unspeakable debauchery, and multiple dead-end jobs, just like my real life!"

> —John Roderick, lead singer/songwriter, The Long Winters

Also by **Bob Powers**

Happy Cruelty Day!

Book One in the
Just Make a Choice! Series

YOU Are a MISERABLE EXCUSE for a HERO!

Bob Powers

Thomas Dunne Books
St. Martin's Griffin ≈ **New York**

THOMAS DUNNE BOOKS.
An imprint of St. Martin's Press.

www.thomasdunnebooks.com
www.stmartins.com

Book design by Greg Collins

Illustrations by Stephen Gardner

Library of Congress Cataloging-in-Publication Data

Powers, Bob, 1973–
    You are a miserable excuse for a hero! / Bob Powers.—1st ed.
        p. cm.— (Just make a choice! series ; bk. 1)
    ISBN-13: 978-0-312-37734-2
    ISBN-10: 0-312-37734-7
    1. Plot-your-own stories. 2. Self-actualization (Psychology)—Fiction.
I. Title.
    PS3616.O8834Y68 2008
    813'.6—dc22   2008009981

10 9 8 7 6 5 4 3 2

A Note on Being in Your Thirties and Having Accomplished Very Little

In this book, YOU get to be the main character in an exciting kidnapping adventure that YOU WANT NO PART OF. You're a thirty-three-year-old struggling actor with VERY LITTLE HOPE of ever being successful, and you feel like time is running out for you to make something of yourself. With every passing day you are that much closer to giving up, and every choice feels weighted with the possibility that it will send you down a path to FAILURE. At thirty-three there's no time left to go back and start over again. So you've been doing your best to make no decisions whatsoever. But lately it's getting a lot harder to keep an even keel.

There are grad school brochures in your bathroom that your ex left in there when she still had hope for you, and you've been flipping through them more often lately. It's getting harder and harder to show up at your waiter job every night. Your friends have all settled into lucrative careers that you resent and fruitful marriages that you envy, while you've done everything you can to commit to nothing for fear of limiting your options. For YOU, as long as you choose to do nothing, ANYTHING is possible.

Enter JULIA! She's the pretty girl you went out with last night and she's been KIDNAPPED! It's up to you and you alone to rescue her. The ensuing adventure will force you to make a series of choices that will not only determine the life or death of an innocent girl, but will force you to

ADD FOCUS to your career and your love life in ways that you've been avoiding ever since you got out of college.

BE VERY CAREFUL! You're DIRECTING THE STORY and the CHOICES you make can result in MURDER, GRADUATE SCHOOL ENROLLMENT, TORTURE, MARRIAGE, POSTAPOCALYPTIC SLAVERY, UNWANTED PREGNANCY, even TEMPING! It's YOUR STORY and YOUR LIFE. All you've got to do is decide which page you want to turn to. *JUST MAKE A CHOICE!!!*

Wake Up, Hero

You awake to the sound of the phone ringing.

"Hello?"

You hear a man's voice. It is muffled. "We've got Julia."

Your head is cloudy with a dream. "Who?"

"Julia, the girl you went out with last night."

Julia, yes, the girl you met at the restaurant the other day. Pretty Julia, with whom just last night you had a delightful first date, followed by a promising first kiss.

"Julia. Yeah. She's great."

"We have her."

"Okay." The dream recedes. "Wait, what do you mean?"

The voice says, "We have kidnapped your girlfriend. If you ever want to see her again—"

"Whoa, she's not my girlfriend," you say. "I just met her. I mean, I had a good time with her and all, but I wanna take it slow with this one, I think."

"We understand," the voice says. "But she's new to the city, and presently, you're all she has. If you ever want to see her again, I suggest you do as we say."

She'd mentioned over drinks that she had just moved from Chicago, but it didn't hit home to you then that she probably has nothing going on for herself yet. Which means she'll be counting on you to be her tour guide and the whole thing will probably get way too serious way too fast. And now you're expected to save her from kidnappers? You might as well just move her into your place and be done with it.

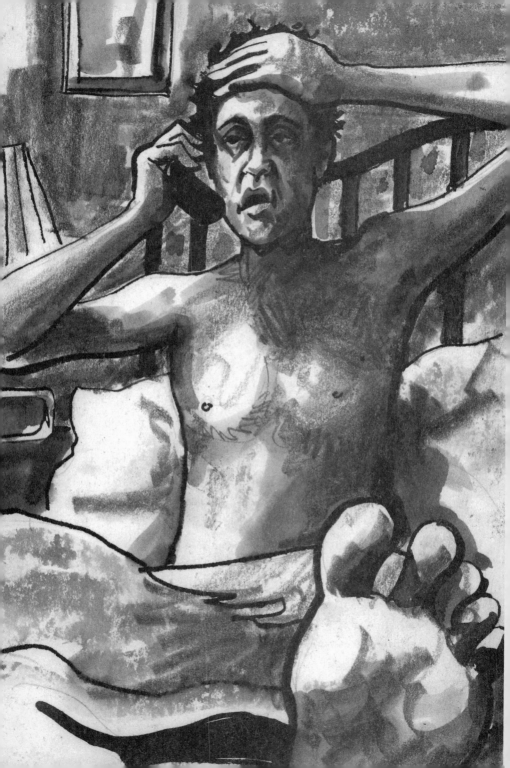

"Look," you say. "Have you told her that you called me?"

The voice asks, "What difference does it make?"

"Well," you say. "If I were to pass on saving her and someone else took care of it, or if your plot was foiled by the cops, then I might still be able to see her again without us having this whole *you saved me from kidnappers* thing forcing us into something really serious."

The voice sighs. "She gave us your number."

Fuck!

"Do you want to talk to her to prove that she's all right?"

"No!" you shout.

The voice speaks more softly. "Look, she heard me ask that. Don't be a dick. I'm gonna put her on."

Your spirit plummets as you listen to the phone change hands.

"Julia?"

She's crying. "I'm so sorry about this. I know it's weird. But honestly, they called everyone else and I had to get them in touch with somebody."

"It's okay," you say. "I understand."

"I just don't want you to think I'm rushing things," she says, panting. "I like you and all. But I've let things get too serious too early on in my past relationships, and I really wanted to take it slow with you. It's just that they've got guns."

There's a rustling as the phone changes hands again.

"Do you want to see Julia again, or not?"

It *was* a good kiss. "What do you want me to do?"

"Give us fifty thousand dollars by tomorrow or we'll blow her head off," the voice says. "We'll call again at midnight with further instructions."

Click.

If you want to go and ask your parents if you can borrow fifty thousand dollars from them, go to page 173.

If you want to have sex with your ex-girlfriend, consider getting back together with her, then think better of it, go to page 183.

WWZBD
(What Would Zack Braff Do?)

With your mind reeling over all the different concerns that are suddenly on your plate, you wander the streets for a while, trying to sort stuff out. Eventually, you come upon a movie theater and buy a ticket for the next movie playing, a Zach Braff film called *She's Trying to Lock Me Up Inside a Little Tiny Box.*

In the darkened theater, you begin to sort through all that's at stake. Julia could very well die if you don't go through with the rescue, no question. But for all you know the kidnapper is planning on murdering you both, in which case the only hope would be to involve the police and leave it to them. But wouldn't that be just another in a long line of cop-outs on your part? With every dilemma in your life, you've always taken the shortest path to doing as little as possible. Maybe it's time you finally did what you know is right, no matter how difficult.

All these divergent thoughts begin to collapse in together and you find yourself getting lost in the movie. Zach Braff's character is about to marry his longtime girlfriend, but he has trouble with commitment so he gets this other girl pregnant who demands that he be a father to her child, but that scares him so he goes on a road trip with his buddies and falls for a girl he meets at a highway tollbooth. She is adorably and irreparably schizophrenic and she just got fired from her job at the tollbooth so she needs a ride back to the hospital. On the way, she gives him some dandelions and teaches him what's really important (the rain, and good hot chocolate). Meanwhile, his rich would-be father-in-law wants him to be a man and take the LSATs, and throughout all of this Zach Braff keeps repeating his catchphrase: "I just wanna watch TV and play my drums!"

"Comb your hair!" you shout at Zach Braff on the screen. You think you're pretty funny, but someone behind you tells you to shush.

Shhhh . . . It sweeps through your head like a gust of wind, clearing away all of the clutter and revealing what it is you have to do. You get up from your seat and walk out of the movie during a montage of Zach Braff and his friends doing cannonballs at a pool where they're trespassing.

If you want to harness your newfound resolve to do the unselfish and heroic thing and go home to await the kidnappers' instructions, go to page 176.

If you just want to spend all the ransom money on Lotto tickets, go to page 16.

Stay Together for America

It should have been easy to make it all go away. All of the kidnappers were dead. There were no living witnesses to the marriage ceremony. Just before your gurneys were lifted into separate ambulances, you and Julia turned your heads on your pillows and looked into each other's eyes, and without needing to say a word you both agreed that you would never speak of the wedding to anyone. You would return to your lives as you left them.

The police came to you first, wanting to know if the kidnappers were a part of some sort of cult. Did they engage in any rituals? Did they make you do things to each other? Did they try to control your minds, or your hearts? Then the police held up the sheets of paper they found on the basement floor, the ones covered in your and Julia's vows of love and devotion for each other, and they wanted to know what the hell happened down there.

It was no more than forty-eight hours before the story swept the nation and suddenly you and Julia were the most beloved couple in the country. Yours was the love held captive, the shotgun wedding of a whole other kind, the couple that was buried alive for nearly half a decade, and when they dug you back up you were newlyweds. It was the most romantic story that had ever graced the cover of *People* magazine, and all that America wanted was for your love to be true.

The public celebration of your marriage was so overwhelming that you and Julia were swept up in it along with the rest of the country, and you decided to give your marriage a shot after all. Unfortunately, after so many years locked away together, the sudden freedom stirred an intense antipathy between the two of you, and any time you were in the same room together you'd start sweating really heavily and Julia would start talking really loudly until she squeezed so tightly on her drinking glass that it broke in her hand. It made your exclusive appearance on *Oprah* a disaster.

When you announced that you would be annulling the marriage, it was as if you were breaking up with America. The press wanted someone to blame, and they chose you. Julia was anointed as America's sweetheart and rumors began to swirl that you had been abusive to her, that you had cheated, that you had been in cahoots with the kidnappers. She spoke in your defense, but that only made them give her more of their love and shower you with ever-increasing hate. It built and built until today, when you make an appearance at a ribbon-cutting ceremony for a new Staples (you need the work). Just after you cut the ribbon, a shot will ring out and you'll find yourself on the ground with a bullet in your chest, all the people running away from you and seeking cover. In an instant, you'll be the only one in the parking lot. The ribbon you just cut will flutter into your line of vision, a snake of red against the blue sky, all of it blurring impossibly to black.

THE END

Vigilantes Do It with a Grudge

When you go and visit your vigilante neighbor for help, he has a drug dealer tied to one of his breakfast chairs. You watch as he slaps at the dealer's arm, then spikes one of his veins with a hypodermic needle full of heroin. The drug dealer shows you the whites of his eyes, then falls quiet into a nod.

"I'm turning this pusher into a doper," your neighbor tells you. "In another week I'll set him free so he can live like all the zombies out there that he helped create."

His utility bills say his name is Ray Stubbins, but after his wife and child were murdered and the police let the killer go free on a technicality, he became a vigilante and changed his name to Ray the Real Rain, as in "the real rain" that's gonna fall one day and wash the streets clean of all the pimps, dopers, pushers, killers, and rapists sending this city to hell one unanswered crime at a time. He likes to be called Rain for short.

Vigilante or not, he's always been a friendly and considerate neighbor to you. Before today, you never knocked on his door for anything more than a cup of sugar.

"There's this girl I like," you tell Rain. "She's been kidnapped. I was hoping you could help me rescue her."

"That's a big cup of sugar," Ray the Real Rain says. He starts asking you lots of questions. Does the kidnapper have a sick kid, and is the girl's dad the CEO of a chemicals company that got the kid sick? Is the girl a senator who cut the funding to the program that provides treatment for the kidnapper's mom's TB? Could the girl be a cokehead and the kidnapper's her cokehead boyfriend and they're just staging this whole thing to get money to buy some more coke? You realize you don't know all that much about Julia, except you're pretty sure she's not a senator.

"And she's really pretty," you say. "Please, Rain. I need someone like you. I don't have what it takes to follow this kind of thing through."

Ray the Real Rain says he can't help you. "I work in black and white. Good and bad. I need to see the obvious injustice that's been done. Love's too gray. You need a love vigilante. Someone who can slit a stranger's throat in the name and defense of true love."

"Where do I find a love vigilante?" you ask.

"You don't find one," Rain says. "You become one. I can show you how, and when you're ready, you will have the dedication required to take out an entire army of kidnappers. But first, you have to be sure that you're in love with this girl and are willing to give yourself completely and totally to that love. Check your heart."

If you want to accept that you are in love with Julia and begin your training, go to page 108.

If you're not sure how you feel about Julia and you want to go home and find some other way of rescuing her before making any big commitment, go to page 116.

There's Always Graduate School

You have a rather inconvenient scheduling conflict. You've got the dinner shift at your waiter job, and the kitchen doesn't stop serving until after midnight. If you want to stay home and wait for the kidnapper's midnight call, you'll first have to call in sick. Not as easy as it sounds.

You wait tables at a place called Lunch Counter, the magical new restaurant where the turkey clubs, pork chops, and omelettes of the traditional American lunch counter are updated with wasabi mayo spreads and cranberry chutney. It's another in a long line of way-too-high concept restaurants that take everyday slop and upgrade it with pricey ingredients to create a kitschy gourmet dining experience. They all fail within three years, but while they're hot you make a lot of money waiting their tables.

You've been feeling as if Lunch Counter is going to be your last restaurant job for a little while now. You used to think your big break was right around the corner and you just had to wait a few more tables before you would be a successful and very well-respected actor who would pick your parts based on how they exercise your craft and not how much they pay, and also you would date Kirsten Dunst briefly but it wouldn't be serious.

Years have passed with very little encouragement from casting directors and the tables in need of waiting have multiplied. An audition feels more like a chore than an opportunity now. You've tried to forge your own path to success by writing a one-person show. It's called *Where YOU Were on 9/11,* and it's an Anna Deveare Smith–style documentary monologue piece in which you interview people about where they were on September 11th and then you perform their stories word for word. You've been developing it for three-and-a-half years now. Unfortunately, you can't find anyone who was in or even near the towers who'll talk to you, and you don't feel like it'll be ready until you do.

You don't dream about overnight success anymore. What you dream of now is getting hit by a city vehicle, like a Parks Department truck or a street sweeper, and losing the use of your legs. The city would pay you a big settlement that would take care of you for life and your friends would gather around your bed shaking their heads in lament for the hugely successful acting career you would most certainly have had if only fate hadn't robbed you of your legs.

You know when you either quit or get fired from your current waiter job you won't have it in you to go find work at another restaurant. Which is why when you call in sick to Lunch Counter tonight and your boss tells you to either show up or you're fired, it's clear to you that saving Julia means finally giving up on your dream of becoming an actor. If you stick it out just a little longer—and just a little longer is all it might take for that big break to finally come around the corner—Julia dies.

If you want to give up on acting so that you can save Julia's life, go to page 57.

If you don't think Julia has the right to expect you to give up on your dream like this, though she surely didn't ask to be kidnapped, and of course she couldn't have known your circumstances or the state of your resolve, but still . . . go to page 179.

And the Man at Table Number Two Feels Nothing

The soldier has just pinned Marie's arm above her head, exposing her bare armpit to the surrounding patrons, all of them cheering and sobbing for the young couple, but the man at table number two appears to feel nothing. When he signals you to bring him his check, he waves his hand in the air, but his eyes remain on the couple writhing on the lunch counter. They look to be all at once craving and relishing each other's touch, the look of lovers disbelieving that such a passion can really be theirs. The man at table number two could just as easily be staring at lawn sprinklers.

He is older, the healthy type who looks about forty-five but could be pushing sixty. He's one of your regulars, always comes in alone, and you're pretty sure his name is James, though you always have to double-check his credit card.

You bring him the bill with his card. His eyes remain on the couple on the lunch counter. You stand beside him, watching with him.

"I was always kind of attracted to her," you say as the two of you watch Marie help her soldier unlace his combat boots.

"Me, too," he says. He signs his bill and hands it to you. "I'm afraid this is good-bye, my friend. I won't be coming back."

"But you come here every week," you say. "I thought you loved eating here."

"I tolerated eating here," he says. "It was her I loved."

He gestures to Marie. Her soldier is shirtless and she is methodically tasting with open-mouth kisses each of the many shrapnel scars littering his torso.

"From the moment I laid eyes on her, I was helpless," he says. "I came back night after night, I tolerated this pretentious menu and obnoxious concept, but it was for her that I hungered. And yet I never bothered to speak a word to her, never even summoned the nerve to sit in her station. I was always afraid of the moment being wrong, of the timing being off, and everything being ruined. I chose to embrace the potential, and dream of the day I would finally give her my love. Tonight I watched that dream obliterate, with great shock and awe, when that hero touched down on his native soil and took hold of what's his. There's nothing left for me here."

"I'm sorry," you say.

James shrugs. "You let enough of your life pass you by, you don't get so rattled after a while. I'm used to it."

"Does it really get easier?" you ask.

James stands and extends his hand. "It starts to feel like everyone around you is a character in a really long movie, and you're the only one in the audience," he says. You shake hands. "You've been a good waiter to me."

"Good-bye, James," you say.

James walks out of the restaurant and you go back to watching Marie and her soldier. He is crying now, and she is kissing his tears. You take a seat, thinking that you could watch this all night long.

THE END

Fifty Thousand Dollars and Not a Dream in Your Head

After several hours of standing around the 7-Eleven drinking Slurpees and eating burritos while listening to the screeching machine issue your fifty thousand Quick Pik Lotto tickets, a reporter named Mia Mendoza runs through the doors and shoves a microphone in your face.

"I guess you woke up feeling lucky today," she says.

You glare at the counterman, assuming that he tipped off the local news that someone was throwing away a shit-load of money in his store. He sheepishly continues to read a pornographic magazine without looking up.

"I woke up with someone depending on me," you say into her microphone. "I'm letting her down." You spot the camera pointed at you and you wonder if Julia has a TV, and whether she'll be able to see this.

Mia Mendoza plows ahead with her next question because she is a hard-nosed reporter who won't stop until she gets her story. "What are you gonna do with all that money if you win?" she asks.

You're still staring into the camera. Mia Mendoza has made it possible for you to show your face to the girl you've chosen to let die. Julia could be watching. They might have given her a TV. Until now, Julia might as well have been hidden away in another dimension. Thanks to Mia Mendoza, she might get the chance to look into your eyes and listen to the Lotto machine's endless dot-matrix cacophony of ticket printing. You could even say something to her if you like.

"Is this live?" you ask Mia.

"Uh-huh!" Mia says. "You wanna tell your boss you won't be coming in tomorrow if one of these tickets hits it big?"

"I was supposed to use this money to pay a ransom to some kidnappers and save an abducted girl's life," you say into the camera. "Instead I spent it on Lotto tickets. The only way I can apologize to her is to let the whole world know that that's the kind of person I am. This is what I'll do if you ask me to be your hero."

The camera stays on the two-shot of you, staring out at the viewer with a "here-but-for-the-grace-of-God-go-you" look, and Mia Mendoza, wearing that smile so beloved and trusted within her tristate area, her lips refusing to let slip even a quiver of uncertainty. She hesitates for just a second, allowing the viewers, and maybe Julia, to feast on the image uncorrupted by words, with the Lotto machine providing the sound track. Then Mia Mendoza throws back to the studio with the grace for which she has earned two local Emmy award nominations.

"It takes all kinds," she says with a flirty shrug. "Back to you, Ron."

If you want to try to alleviate the guilt by going to Gamblers Anonymous meetings, go to page 187.

If you want to live with the guilt and drop-out of your life and go sell candles and shit like that, go to page 50.

Show Us Your Wipe Face!

You and Danny came up with the idea for Wipe-face.com during one of your many late-night drinking binges after a shift waiting tables at Tots, the briefly trendy restaurant (since shuttered) that featured high-end elementary-school cafeteria food (menu specialties included mahimahi fish sticks, peppercorn-encrusted Salisbury steak, and their famous $44 plate of tater tots dusted with truffle shavings). Drunk on all the liquor each night's tips could buy, you and Danny would spend hours slurring out concepts for what you each dreamed would be the hot new billion-dollar Web property to lift you out of your jobs waiting tables and turn you both into moguls.

"Hypochondriac dot com," you'd bark while Danny wrote. "The place where hypochondriacs can go to describe their imagined symptoms and post their time-lapse photos of moles changing shape and color and stuff, and other hypochondriacs can rate on a scale of one to ten how much cancer they have based on the photos. And the home page would have big letters that read NO LICENSED MEDICAL PHYSICIANS ALLOWED!!!"

"Okay, here's one," Danny would slur in turn. "Momfights dot com. You post a photo of your mom on the site, and then visitors vote on which mom looks more nurturing."

And you'd go on like that until last call. It was during one of these nights that one of you mumbled over the rim of his glass the idea for Wipe-face.com, a place where users would post photos of the faces they make while wiping their asses. The slogan would be "Show Us Your Wipe Face!"

It was sheer chance that Danny bothered to write the idea down, and even more of a miracle that he managed to hang onto the napkin he wrote on without blowing his nose or wiping the mysterious blood from his lip on the drunken bus ride home.

Most miraculous of all, after countless nights of spewing these silly ideas at each other, Danny actually followed through on that one. He registered the domain for Wipe-face and launched a rudimentary Web site. He had asked you early on if you wanted to be his partner and chip in $75 for the Web-hosting service. You hemmed and hawed on getting him the cash, and eventually you just started chastising him for wasting his time on a stupid Web site idea.

"That would just be a distraction," you said, though you really had no projects from which to be distracted. You simply preferred to avoid failure by not trying in the first place, and you wanted your friends to take the same route so that you could all stay at the same level of non-success forever and ever. Maybe you could all open a bar together, or a boxing gym for inner-city kids.

Wipe-face became a viral Web sensation and Danny became a multimillionaire. You haven't spoken to him since. You can't think about him, or the Web site, without getting nauseous over how stupid you were. For quite some time you found that even the act of wiping your ass would fill you with regret. Visiting him today will not be easy.

When you settle into Danny's office, he invites you to take an iPod from the pile sitting in the corner. "I don't even know where they come from. They just get sent to me, and I run out of room," he says. You decline the iPod.

"I need your help, Danny," you say. "A girl's been kidnapped and I need fifty thousand dollars for the ransom."

Danny gets up from his desk and turns to watch the baby sharks swim around the embedded tank that composes the entire back wall of his office. Two of the sharks are eating a water snake.

"I was hurt that you cut me off after my Web site got successful," Danny says, his back still to you. "You were my friend. You were supposed to be happy for me."

"I wanted to be," you say.

"Well, at least you have a girl in your life now," Danny says. He pulls out his checkbook. "Success or not, it's pretty great to see you throw all you have at something."

He writes a check and holds it out to you. When you reach to take it, he yanks it back.

"I don't want you to disappear from my life again. The conditions of me giving you this money are as follows. You never pay me back, as long as you come here and work for me. For one year. Nine to five."

Working nine to five would require that you stop auditioning, and considering how old you are, it would be tantamount to finally giving up on acting. There's a big part of you that is excited to have the excuse to finally give it up. The other part of you is pissed that Danny would ever put you in a position that requires that you give up on your dream in order to do what's right, especially considering how hard it is for you to even be in this office. That part of you wants to tell Danny to go fuck himself.

"I still love you," Danny says. "But I'm still real pissed that you stopped being my friend. I can't just give you fifty grand and have you drop out of my life again. What's it gonna be?"

If you want to accept the money and come work for Danny, go to page 143.

If you want to tell Danny you'll find the money someplace else, go to page 55.

The Finish Line Is Just the Beginning

You've been to the finish line of a marathon before. It always looks like the scene of an international incident. Everyone is emaciated, covered in their own waste, their thighs ripped open from the chafing with blood pooling at the tops of their sneakers, all of them writhing on the ground in pain while volunteers force water and citrus down their throats to keep them from dying or succumbing to madness. For charity.

Today is no different. Women and men are all over the street, writhing and hugging and holding up poster-size pictures of mothers and sisters they've lost. You're careful to position yourself away from the path of the runners, afraid that one might come flailing into you and scream for any salt tablets you might have on your person.

"PSSSST!"

The sound is very loud and pronounced and you turn around to find its source.

"PSSSST!"

Loud as a bullet whizzing past your ear.

"PSSSST!"

Finally you spot a man with his face hidden under a black hood standing behind a water kiosk, impatiently shooting air between his teeth at you. You go to him.

"Chet," you say.

"Stop calling me that," he says through the hood.

You notice the HI, MY NAME IS CHET sticker on his tee shirt but you refrain from calling his attention to it.

"You don't exactly blend in with the hood on," you say.

"The black hoods represent the dead claimed by the

disease," Chet says. "Look around."

You scan the crowd and find dozens of people wearing black hoods. You see a volunteer handing them out to new arrivals.

"And yes," Chet says. "Some of those hoods are my associates. They are watching us closely."

You are frightened when a runner flails herself against the plywood of Chet's kiosk with enough force that he has to steady himself to keep the whole structure from tipping over. He quickly unscrews a bottle of vitaminwater and thrusts it into the runner's writhing hands.

When the runner leaves, you say to Chet, "So this is just a convenient cover for the drop-off? Pretty coldhearted."

You can tell by the look in his eyes that Chet is personally offended. He says he volunteers at the marathon every year. He starts barking statistics at you, how many die of breast cancer each year, how little funding is being allocated.

"Maybe you should think a little more about others for a change," Chet says. "Now, do you have the money or are we going to have to kill your girlfriend?"

You show Chet your father's check for $50,000.

"What the fuck am I supposed to do with that?" Chet asks.

"I could sign it over to you," you say.

"Cash," Chet says. "Go to the bank and come back here with fifty grand in green, or your girlfriend gets it."

If you want to go to the bank and try to cash your father's check, go to page 68.

If you want to demand that Chet show you that Julia is all right first, go to page 161.

The Man Behind the Curtain Is So Fucking Bored

You yank the tape from a video cartridge and use it to tie Deke to a chair, then you start hitting him in the face with stuff (a pencil sharpener, a box of Kleenex, some mail), warning him that you won't stop until he tells you where the kidnapper is. Suddenly, the room is illuminated when the TV monitors lining the wall come to life. A man is on the screen. He has your face.

"Thank you, Deke," he says. "I won't need your services anymore."

That's your face on the screen. It's pale and gaunt. But it's your face.

"Hello, Brother," the man says. "Didn't know you were a twin, did you?"

You certainly did not. Your parents wanted to keep it that way, as the man in the TV goes on to explain.

Since he was born second, your parents assumed he was the evil twin, so they named him Josiah and kept him locked in the attic for eighteen years. That's why his skin is so white and translucent, revealing the blood flowing through his veins like so many black snakes racing through his body. You ask him what it was like.

"It sucked ass," Josiah says. "But in between the flagellations and the scalding hot-water baptisms, our parents had their moments of mercy when they'd give me the only thing I craved: news about you."

They showed him your report cards and your class pictures. On the rare occasion when you won a trophy for honorable mention or "Good Sport," your parents would sneak it up to the attic to let Josiah hold it to his chest and imagine that it was his achievement that had earned such an honor. On his, and your, birthday, they'd carry him out of the attic and into your room late at night to let him watch you sleep for a few minutes, when he'd marvel at how much you'd grown. On Christmas, after you'd unwrapped all of your presents and had fallen asleep from all the excitement, your parents would climb the stairs to the attic to tell Josiah all the things you'd been given and how much fun you had playing with them.

"One time," Josiah says, "they even snuck down to the rec room while you were making out with Danielle, your high school girlfriend, and they snatched her bra from the floor and let me hold it in my fingertips. I clutched that lace and thrilled for you and your conquest."

"You lived through me," you say.

"No," he says. "You lived *for* me. You had my face, my biology, and you lived the life I would have lived if our parents hadn't thought I'd been born evil."

After you both turned eighteen and you went off to college, your parents wanted to turn the attic into an exercise room, so they set Josiah free, providing him with a very generous trust fund on the condition that he would never report them to the cops. It was his big chance to make his own life, but he had been living vicariously through you for so long that he didn't want to stop. So he hired Deke to install a surveillance system in your home, and Josiah spent the past decade tracking your movements and being audience to your every decision, your every achievement, and your every milestone.

"Holy *shit,* that was boring!" he says. "It's like you were the one living in the attic. You shrank from every opportunity, gave up on every project, and aborted every relationship just to avoid investing anything of yourself. I couldn't believe it when you broke it off with Kim! She was a fucking charity worker to put up with your shit for so long. I felt like I was at a horror movie, screaming at the fucking screen, *Don't do it, you fucking moron! She's all you've got!* When you started up with this Julia here, I couldn't take it anymore. I had to kidnap her."

"To protect her?" you ask.

"To get you to do something!" he says. "To make you devote yourself to something more than waking up every morning and making an excuse."

"Like you're so much better," you say. "You spent the last decade watching someone else's life instead of living your own."

"I was locked in an attic for eighteen years, asshole," he says. "I spent my childhood getting into loud arguments with spiders. What's your excuse?"

"Maybe I could sense that I had a twin, and I felt like I wasn't able to give my all to anything because a big part of me was locked away someplace."

Looking into your brother's eyes, you know your days of making excuses are over. Those are your eyes, tinted red from so many years straining in darkness. His eyes are furious. Yours begin to form tears.

"I'm sorry I let you down for so long."

"It was worth it," he says. "You're a hero now. It's not everyone who gets to say he has a hero for a brother. Now go rescue that girlfriend of yours."

He gives you the address of the house where you'll find Julia, safe and sound. The kidnappers holding her will be instructed to let her go. Then your brother says good-bye, since he has to go into hiding because he'll be wanted for kidnapping.

"It's an honor to be your brother," he says. Then the TVs go black, and you take off running to the address and save the girl.

You marry Julia and you try to live the best life you can live. You live the life your brother would want you to live, just in case he's watching.

THE END

An Abortion in Time for Happy Hour

You shove Kim across the front seat and drive as fast as you can across town to the abortion clinic. You explain to Kim that you're not trying to get out of saving Julia, you just don't need this added pressure of worrying about how what happens today could make or break the personality development of an innocent unborn child. Kim says that if you can make it in time and they'll take her, she'll get the abortion because she would not ever want to have the child of a man who would conduct his life in this manner.

"The sooner I can get your DNA out of my body, the better," she says. "Step on it."

You comply. After running several red lights and breaking numerous speed limits, you skid to a stop out front of the abortion clinic just as the old Italian man inside flips the CLOSED sign on the door. You both jump from the car and start pounding on the glass for him to let you in.

The old Italian man opens the door a crack and says, "We closed already! You come'a back early tomorrow. I give'a you abortion then."

You and Kim beg him to open up. "Just one more, sir. It won't take long. Please."

The old Italian man throws his hands in the air and says, "You kids want everything this'a very minute. I'm not your Internet. You'a want abortion, you come'a back in the morning. I take'a you first thing."

He slams the door shut in your face. You continue to shout through the glass for him to open up, but he just

walks into the back, muttering to himself about how impatient kids are when they want to have an abortion. You watch him turn off the lights, lift his sleeping house cat into his arms, and go up the steps to his apartment above the clinic.

If you want to climb onto the fire escape to knock on the old Italian abortionist's window, go to page 141.

If you want to find out what life would have been like if you'd never been born, go to page 137.

A Good Kidnapper Is a Patient Kidnapper

The kidnappers contact your dad to get more ransom out of him, but he says that his divorce from your mom is really complicating things, and it's going to take a little time.

"We will wait," Chet tells you through his hood. You still haven't seen any of their faces, and they are determined that you never will. "I take my work as a kidnapper very seriously. The man who hired us to kidnap you is paying us handsomely, regardless of whether we receive the ransom or not. We'll wait years if we have to. You don't leave until our demands are met."

The next four years of captivity pass without too many wrinkles. You and Julia spend the first few months having lots of superhot, "we-could-die-at-any-minute" type sex. Then things calm down in the relationship and you're able to concentrate on other pursuits, such as waiting for meals or counting silently.

The second year seems to fly by because that's the year they give you the board game Othello, which is a really fun game (and you're relieved to discover that Julia is far from a novice at the ol' "moor board").

During your third year in the basement, the bloom fades from the rose and the effects of constantly being in the same room together start to wear on you. You find that you can't touch Julia anymore without her skin erupting with a moist, unsightly rash at the exact spot where your bare skin came in contact with hers. Julia stops talking to you completely after you develop a tic wherein the sound of her voice makes you fall to the ground screaming, unable to stop until you grow hoarse. You both begin to worry that maybe the only reason you're still together is because the men outside have guns and they'll shoot you if you try to go. You always knew that was a big part of what you saw in each other, but there used to be something more than that.

Near the end of the third year, you and Julia warm to each other again, and it feels just like it did at the beginning, except with a little more wisdom. You spend the bulk of your fourth year cuddling in love. You start to think that if you ended up staying in that basement until you die, it wouldn't be so bad. At least, not until Julia says, "We need to start making better use of our time."

She begins obsessing over all of the years she's losing and how far behind she'll be when the two of you get out. At first she took a lot of notes on the experience, hoping to write a book when she got out so her journalism degree would not have gone to waste. But the notes started getting pretty repetitive after not too long.

She tries to convince the kidnappers to let you take correspondence courses at the continuing ed. and graduate level while you're being held captive. They go along with the idea, and they give you some course books from the local community college. Julia starts pressuring you to map out a course load for yourself, so you circle a random selection of philosophy and literature courses.

"You have to be more practical!" she says. "We've already lost a huge chunk of our thirties. Wouldn't it be great if you had a useful degree when we got out?"

"*If* we get out!" you reply. You're surprised by the

hopefulness in your voice. You realize then how scared you are of having to live a free life and make your own choices again.

The schooling idea gets tossed once the kidnappers discover you'll need to use a computer to take classes online. So Julia starts asking if you and she can get married instead.

"I already asked Chet and he said Marcus, the tall kidnapper, is a justice of the peace. Chet, Sam, and Reggie can be witnesses."

"I don't even know if they can be legitimate witnesses since we've never even seen their faces," you say. "Can't this wait until we get out?"

"*If* we get out," she says. "I want to stop waiting until later to live my life. Let's live now. Let's get married."

If you want to marry Julia, go to page 62.

If you want to be tempted by the charms of another, go to page 190.

In the Arms of Reggie

"**Please take your** hood off," you whisper to Reggie. "Pleeease?"

"Against the rules," Reggie whispers. "If they knew you could ID me they'd probably kill me."

"Just one little peek," you coo. "I want to see your beautiful face."

"You have my mouth," Reggie says.

"I do," you giggle. "And I'm not going to ever give it back."

"Will you two shut the fuck up?" Julia barks from the bed.

"Sorry," you and Reggie say in unison from the floor.

She was stung that you would leave her in favor of a man who keeps his face hidden under a black hood and who has kept you locked in a basement for the past four years. In the weeks that followed the breakup, she's been really cranky, especially since all three of you now have to share the basement together every night.

"As captive," Julia told Reggie during one of their fights, "I have a right to this space. You belong upstairs, where the captors live. What do they think you're doing down here every night anyway?"

"Raping you," he said to Julia.

She laughed. "Me!"

Reggie looked to you. "I'm not out to them. I'm not sure how they'd take it."

Julia continued to laugh at Reggie. He looked wounded. You rubbed his arm and said to Julia, "Everyone should be allowed to pick his own time to come out! You should be more understanding."

It was the first and last time you took his side in one of their fights. It pushed her over the edge. She's been ice cold to you ever since, speaking only to tell you and Reggie when you're getting on her nerves, or when she has something urgent to say.

"I'm escaping," Julia tells you after Reggie has gone upstairs for the day. It takes you a moment to get past the surprise that she's actually speaking to you before you discern the meaning of what she just said.

"I considered not telling you," she goes on. "But I knew you'd be too happy to have Reggie all to yourself that you wouldn't rat me out. Also, I wanted to give you the chance to come with me."

The nausea starts to percolate in your stomach. "You'll get caught," you tell her.

"I won't," she says without missing a beat. The certainty in her voice makes you believe her.

"If this is just to get me back—"

"I don't want you back. I want my life back. And I'm offering you a chance to have yours back," she says. "If you really love Reggie, and if he really loves you, he'll be happy to let you go and live your life. You'll find each other on the outside and you'll be able to see how you are out in the real world, free to lead your lives and pursue your dreams."

You try to remember what it was like to have a life to

live as you wish, what it meant to choose when and what you'll eat every day, to decide how to pass your time and what goals to pursue. You know you're supposed to want all of that, but you can't help feeling terrified.

"Will you come with me?" Julia asks.

If you want to escape with Julia, go to page 52.

If you want to let her go without you, go to page 135.

Good Cop, Sucky Cop

You're sitting on your couch facing Officer Cortez, the man you spoke to on the phone, and Officer Frank, his partner. Officer Cortez is a good cop who just wants to serve the community and do his part to make the city a better place. Officer Frank has been rather abrasive ever since he let a kidnap victim die in 2003 when he called a kidnapper's bluff and raided the hideout instead of meeting their demands.

"I think we should ignore their demands and call their bluff," Officer Frank says to his partner.

You ask, "Isn't that the way you botched your first kidnapping rescue?"

Officer Frank snaps that that first time was just a fluke and what the hell do you know about police work anyway.

Cortez asks Frank to step outside for a second.

When it's just the two of you, Officer Cortez confides that he isn't sure Officer Frank's strategy is the wisest, but he has to let his partner do it his way if he's ever going to absolve himself of the guilt he feels for letting a girl die.

"Besides, I haven't seen him this excited in forever," Officer Cortez says. "You're really helping my partner let go of the past tonight, pal. I thank you for that. And if we save your girlfriend, I'm gonna thank her, too."

"What do you mean 'if'?" you ask. "Isn't there another way to do this?"

Officer Cortez says, "There is. But it would require a whole lot more effort on your part. You up for it?"

If you are up for it, go to page 75.

If you want to just let them use Officer Frank's strategy and hope that Julia doesn't die, go to page 103.

Six Months of Leon

Six months after Leon's improbable and highly publicized rescue of Julia (it was all over the papers, LOVERS REUNITED IN DARING KIDNAP RESCUE), you give Julia a call and you and she meet for lunch. Any hopes you have of her breaking it off with Leon are dashed the minute she waddles through the door.

"So how far along are you?" you ask.

"Six months," Julia says, her hands caressing her round belly. "It's been such a transformation for me. I never thought I could care so much for another living thing."

You wait for your appetizers in awkward silence. Julia sips her hot water with lemon and her eyes light up like she's tasting a bowl of melted chocolate. You sip from your Maker's Mark and Diet Coke. It's a bit flat.

"You seem really happy," you say. "Have you thought of a name yet?"

"Leon, if it's a boy," she says. "And if it's a girl . . ."

"Leona."

"Yes!" she says. "It just seems like the right thing. It's almost like that kidnapping was meant to happen, so that I could find out just how much Leon cares for me. Watching him creep into the safe house and snap the necks of my abductors, one after the other, like a procession of death, silent and solemn. I was suddenly amazed that I had ever said no to this man whose love for me is so unwavering, so precise and absolute. And I got pregnant almost immediately, like our baby was spawned from the kidnapping."

She leans across the table, as if she has a secret to share.

"Do you know that feeling, when it seems like all these

wild events are coming together solely to effect a big change in your own life?"

"Totally," you lie.

Your lunch arrives and you eat while Julia tells you about her wedding ceremony, jokingly referring to it as "our shotgun wedding," even though it was at a villa in Tuscany. She tells you about her new column in a parenting magazine, which she was given after she wrote a firsthand account of the kidnapping and subsequent pregnancy and marriage for a respectable local glossy. The column is called "Adventure Mom," and there's already talk of a book. She repeats over and over again how glad she is to get together with you after all that craziness she put you through. When she asks you what you've been up to, you deflect the question by asking whether she plans to raise the baby in any particular religion, and she says Episcopalian.

THE END

Your Dad Is Way Controlling

When you come out of the bank after cashing Danny's check, a nearby pay phone starts to ring. You pick it up. It's the kidnapper.

"Tonight at midnight," the kidnapper says. "The old abandoned ketchup factory on the outskirts of town. Bring the money."

When you hang up, a car screeches up to the curb. Your dad is behind the wheel and he's holding up a brief-case.

"Get in!" he says. "I got your ransom money."

"How'd you find out about the kidnapping?" you ask.

"Kim called us," he says. "She was worried about you. I got the money. Let's go!"

"But I got it myself, Dad," you say. You hold up the bag of cash the bank gave you. It's burlap and there's a big dollar sign on it.

Your dad looks at the bag and his face goes white. His little thirty-three-year-old boy is all growed up. You're finding your own way, getting yourself out of jams, figuring out how to round up fifty grand in cash on twenty-four hours' notice. It's clear from the look in his eyes that your dad is terrified. If he doesn't have a screw-up son to bail out of stuff anymore, what's he got left?

"Save that for your next girlfriend's kidnapping," he says. "Now get in the car."

"I wanted to do this by myself," you say.

"But why?" he asks, truly bewildered.

To be honest, you're not really sure. "I just think I'm supposed to?"

He's desperate when he shouts, "You'll screw it up!"

He looks like he wants to suck the words back in. He's waiting for you to say something, to let him know whether he blew it, whether he's lost you forever.

You don't really disagree with him. You almost want to let him take over just out of habit. But things have been going pretty well so far. All you have to do is deliver the money and you're a hero. You kind of want to go through with it just out of curiosity, to see if this might be the thing you actually come through on.

But then again, your dad is right there, and he really seems sure that you're gonna blow this. Maybe you should let him handle it.

If you want to tell your dad it's time for you to stand on your own two feet, go to page 126.

If you want to get in the car, go to page 78.

Honor Thy Father by Keeping Thy Mother Away from the Guy She Actually Gave a Shit About

After telling Herbert that you won't give him your mom, you take off and try to flag down a car that will give you a ride to the ransom drop. A few cars pull over, but none of them are comfortable driving you to an abandoned ketchup factory. Finally a man in a U-Haul agrees to take you.

You're too late. There's no one in the factory. You ride around back in the U-Haul, but there's no sign of anyone. The kidnappers are gone. Julia is as good as dead.

"I'd take you back home," the U-Haul driver says. "But this is a one-way rental. I already said good-bye to what's behind me. You can either go where I'm goin' or you can stay put."

Staying put means telling your dad you blew the rescue and squandered his pride. It means going on living like a grown-up child, waiting for him to save you. You did the right thing by your dad in saying no to Herbert. Do right by him again and show him his son can live with his own mistakes.

The U-Haul driver says he's headed out West and he's leaving a whole lot of hurt behind. That sounds like a pretty good plan. You climb into the cab and the two of you take off down the highway, Arizona bound.

THE END

Good-bye, Daddy

"Looks like I get to start making those decisions sooner rather than later, huh, Dad?" you say. "Except, it's still you who's making this decision. Because the only way I know how to handle myself in life is to ask myself, *What would my dad do?* Well, I know for certain that you'd do the right thing, and you wouldn't let an innocent young girl die, would you, Dad?"

Your dad starts freaking out and trying to scream, but his mouth is gagged so it doesn't really bother you.

"Kind of funny, isn't it? I always wanted to show you the kind of man I can be. The kind of man who can make the tough decisions and live with them. And here I finally get to show you that, and you have to die right afterward. Well, Dad, I hope in the split second between the gun going off and the bullet entering your brain, you find the time to be proud of me. I love you, Dad."

You look to Chet and say, "Kill my father."

Chet points a gun at your dad, who is now screaming into his gag. "You want to give him a chance to say something?" Chet asks.

"I suppose he just wants to have one last chance to tell me what to do," you say. "But it won't be any use. I've made up my mind, and going back now would be the greatest shame of my life. Ungag him. Nothing he says can sway me."

Your dad continues shouting gibberish into the gag until Chet yanks it from his mouth. He flinches from the pain,

spits once on the ground, then shouts, "There's another fifty thousand dollars in the car, dumbass!"

Chet turns to you for confirmation.

"Oh yeah," you say.

The ride home is awkward. Your dad drives, with you in the passenger seat and Julia in the back. They both want nothing more than to get away from you.

"I just feel like I owe you something now," Julia says when you walk her to her door. "Like if we ever got serious, any time we disagreed on anything, you'd be able to lord this whole 'I was ready to shoot my dad in the face for you' thing over me. Plus, you being so into me like that, it's really gross."

When you get back to the car, your dad has locked the door. You knock on the window and he rolls it down partway.

"I'd drive you home," he says. "But I wouldn't want to be overly controlling and give you any more reason to have me shot in the face."

Your dad peels away. You turn around to Julia's house and her porch light switches off. You try to decide whether to take a bus home or call a cab, but in the end you choose neither and start walking.

THE END

He Was Supposed to Make
It All Better

Your dad has always told you that if you try to do anything on your own, you'll probably screw it up and that you should just let him handle everything. So when the kidnappers call out for a second time to bring the money into the factory, you stay put. He said he'll make it all better, so you'd just better let him.

"You have one more chance," the kidnapper shouts. "I'll give you ten seconds to bring the money to us, or your dad and your girlfriend are goners."

I hope Dad comes up with a way out of this in ten seconds, you think. Also, she's not my girlfriend, you also think. Then you hear a gunshot.

"That was your girlfriend," the kidnapper shouts. "Still don't think we're serious? Ten more seconds, and your dad's dead."

You count to ten silently in your head. When you reach ten, you're thankful not to hear a gunshot. A few seconds pass, then the kidnapper shouts, "Look, idiot, just bring us the money! Your dad's still alive. He says the money's in the car and you should just bring it to us and this will all be over."

You don't move.

"Your girlfriend's alive, too," the kidnapper shouts, really impatiently now. "We were bluffing. Just bring us the money. Jesus!"

You stay put. That strategy has kept everyone alive thus far so you stick with it. Eventually, the kidnappers come out of the factory pointing their guns at your dad and Julia, whose hands are bound behind their backs. They all walk toward your car with incredulous looks on their faces.

"Just give us the money!" the head kidnapper says when they reach the car. You don't do anything, so they hold a gun on you while they open the doors and reach in to grab the two bags of cash. Then they untie your dad and Julia.

"I don't know what you did to raise him like this," the kidnapper says to your dad. "But Jesus, he sucks!"

The kidnappers go back to the factory and disappear. Your dad and Julia stand by the car, staring in at you as if they came back to their car and found a peacock sitting inside. You look at them and smile. They're both safe. Just like your dad said, everything's all better.

THE END

You Sell Candles and Shit Like That Now

You own and operate a store that sells candles and shit like that now. It's called Straight Outta Ecuador, and in addition to all the different kinds of candles, you sell a whole bunch of garish little figurines (many of them erotic, and many more of them slightly racist looking, even though they probably aren't) and itchy blankets. All the items in the store say on the handwritten price tags that they were made in Ecuador, so college-educated people between the ages of eighteen and twenty-eight buy the living shit out of them.

You started working there not long after you gave the news broadcast about letting Julia die for the sake of playing the Lotto. You had to quit your job at the restaurant because customers refused to let you bring them their food. You gave up on acting after you got kicked out of the various workshops you took part in; no one knew how to direct your performances except to say, "Try it with a little less heartlessness this time." And casting directors would dismiss you from auditions with "Sorry, we're looking for someone who has the capacity to feel empathy for another human being."

You ended up answering the ad for a job at Straight Outta Ecuador. At the time it was still being run by Jasper, a man with a long gray ponytail who dressed only in loose tunics. Jasper claimed not to care about what you did to Julia since he lived his life according to "the morality of the lions," though he never explained what that meant. After a couple years working at the store, Jasper disappeared.

He later sent a letter claiming that he had to go back to Ecuador because he had some "unfinished business" with a medicine man that had apparently fucked him over when he was a younger man (Jasper stole one of the Medicine Man's wives so the Medicine Man slipped Jasper a poison that left him paralyzed from the waist up for fifteen years). In the letter Jasper bequeathed the store to you and gave you the Web site of the Des Moines–based wholesaler where he gets all of his stock (www.indiginous-liquidators.net).

The store provides you with a comfortable living. Though you maintain contact with no one from your past, you still get reminded of Julia on a daily basis. At least one customer a day recognizes you and tells you that you are a monster with a standing reservation for the best table in all of Hell. You let him spill his vitriol all over your checkout counter. Then you say, "You're absolutely right. Now would you still like to buy your candles and your little erotic figurines that appear slightly racist but you're pretty sure aren't?"

The indignant customer always ends up buying your wares. He needs those candles and those little erotic figurines if he wants people who visit his apartment to think that he has interests. And when the customer leaves your store you say to him, "Thank you," and you mean it. Not just because he made a purchase, but because he didn't allow you to forget. He reminded you to revel in your loneliness and your shattered dreams as just punishment for the monstrous act you committed when someone asked you for your help so many years ago.

THE END

Let Jeff Do the Choosing

When Marcus brings you your dinner, Julia smacks him on the back of the head with a footstool, knocking him out cold. Then the two of you sneak upstairs and out of the house. You run for the woods, hoping to hit a road eventually. Julia slips down a ravine and gets injured along the way, but you both keep running.

You make it to the highway where a man picks you both up in his truck. He notices that Julia's leg is torn open and realizes she needs medical attention. "I can take you to this cult that I belong to," he says. "There's a doctor there."

He turns down a back road and drives through the woods until he comes to a sign that reads, JEFF'S CULT, NEXT RIGHT. He makes the turn and in a few minutes you pull into a large compound lined with cabins and bunkhouses. People come outside and carry Julia away. You're led to an empty bunkhouse where you immediately fall asleep.

When you wake up, a man with a gorgeous smile is sitting next to your bed. "Hey, I'm Jeff," he says. "Really great to meet you. You wanna join my cult?"

You tell him you're skeptical, so he shows you a brochure printed out from a color printer and stapled together. It shows cult members engaged in a variety of different activities, all of them wearing shirts that read JEFF'S CULT on the front and BECAUSE JEFF SAID SO on the back. In the photos they're playing volleyball, canoeing, and in one picture they're all eating tacos.

"Taco Sundays," Jeff says when he sees you lingering over the picture of the tacos.

"Every Sunday?" you ask.

"Until I say otherwise," Jeff says, still wearing that magnetic smile.

"What do I have to do?" you ask.

Jeff laughs, "Whatever I tell you to do."

"I mean, do I have to believe in a giant spaceship coming to take us away or anything?"

Jeff's smile now seems to find you absolutely adorable. You blush.

"Giant spaceship? Not right now, no. But who knows, if in a year or two I get all nutty and decide that a giant spaceship is coming to take us away, you'll believe in a giant spaceship."

You ask him about Julia. He tells you she's fine and that he was excited to learn that she's a reporter. He needs someone to write for the cult's daily paper, *Stuff Jeff Said Yesterday*. You ask him to take you to her.

In the medical office, Julia runs to Jeff and they start making out. Then she sees you. "Did you hear about Taco Sundays?" she asks. Then to Jeff, "You know, he's an actor."

"Hey, we could use an actor. I wrote a one-person show about 9/11 and I've been looking for someone to perform," Jeff says, still with that smile. "It's about how 9/11 was my fault because I didn't have enough time to give my love to the whole world. So how about it? You wanna join my cult or what? All you have to do is give up all free will and let me make all your decisions for you."

You think for a second. "Okay, Jeff," you say. "I'm in."

"Congratulations," Jeff says. "That's the last decision you'll *ever* have to make."

Jeff sends you outside to help dig a latrine while he

impregnates Julia. You spend the rest of the day digging
into the ground side by side with your fellow cult members,
wondering if they feel just as light and unburdened as you
feel. At long last, you finally know without a doubt what
you're supposed to do with your life. You're supposed to
dig a latrine. Jeff said so.

THE END

You Can't Put a Price on Bitterness

You explain to Danny that ever since he got successful, he has existed as a living, breathing monument to all the opportunities you never bothered to pursue. Any time you felt like things were going okay and you were feeling pleased with your station in life, you could remember that somewhere out there, Danny was enjoying the vast and unknowable wealth that could have been yours if you had only been willing to invest just the slightest bit of your time and money in something.

"It's not about the job," you say. "It's that I don't want to jeopardize our relationship. If I came in here and saw you every day and we had all of these regular, commonplace interactions, I'd start to miss that featureless, monolithic totem to all of my bitterness and resentment in the world. You've been like my beacon, Danny. No matter where I was or how I was feeling, I just had to turn my thoughts to you and I would be bathed in the bright light of self-loathing. And now you want me to come in and open your mail? I'm sorry, Danny, but you're way more important to me than that."

Danny looks as if he might weep. "Jesus, all this time I just thought you had erased me from your life."

"In a certain way, Danny," you say, "you are my life. Now I'd better get going because being here makes me want to start throwing up and never stop."

"Just one question," Danny says. "Why didn't you go in on the site with me? Sure, it was a long shot, but there was so little investment required. Are you that afraid of failure?"

"I'd be fine with failure," you say. "If I was a failure right now, that'd sit perfectly well with me. It's being a failure six months from now that I can't handle. Or two years from now. It takes too long to find out you're a failure. I'd rather enjoy the fruits of not having tried at all, which are right at my fingertips."

You get up from your chair. Danny grabs your arm and shoves the check in your hand.

"Take it," he says. "I would have paid triple that to learn that I was still important to you."

If you want to take the check, go to page 42.

If you want to tell Danny you can't take the check, go to page 89.

Be the Money Shot

After you decide to stay home from work so you can wait for the kidnappers to call, effectively losing your waiter job and giving up on your acting career, you go through your mail until you find a manila envelope with no return address and no postage on it—just your name, and the words *Open Immediately.*

You rip open the envelope to find a DVD inside. Written in Sharpie on the face of the DVD is a date. Today's date. You put the DVD into your player and press Play.

The image on the screen is you, asleep in bed earlier this morning. You watch yourself wake up and answer the phone. It's a video recording of you getting the ransom call from the kidnapper.

There's clearly a surveillance camera somewhere in your apartment. You're probably being watched right now. You search the walls and light fixtures, feeling your way around the surfaces and in the cracks, but you find nothing that looks like a camera.

You go back to the television. On the recording, you've hung up the phone now and you're just lying in bed, worrying over what to do next. You check the envelope and fish out a little slip of loose-leaf paper. The handwritten note reads:

This isn't about the money. It isn't about the girl. It's about you.

Terrified, you look at the video on the television again. In the video, your hand is under the blanket and you're starting to masturbate halfheartedly. You turn the TV off before you have to watch yourself really go to town.

If you want to track down whoever made this recording, go to page 158.

If you're curious about what it's like to watch yourself masturbate and you want to press Play again, go to page 131.

Your Baby's Daddy Ain't No Coward

You bend down and talk into Kim's stomach.

"Hey, little guy," you say. "I sure can't wait to meetcha. But right now Daddy's got something he's got to take care of. There's a girl that needs some saving. And you can count on your daddy to make sure she gets saved."

You kiss Kim's belly. Then you stand up, and before you realize what's happening, Kim kisses your lips.

"I'm gonna make that baby proud," you say.

"We'll be waiting here for you when you get back," Kim says.

That night, you get the call to bring the money to the abandoned ketchup factory on the outskirts of town. When you get to the drop spot, it's empty. There's not a soul there, and there's no information for where to go next. You're terrified that Julia has been hurt, and you have to keep looking until you find her if you ever want to be a father to your child. That was the deal!

Five years pass with you searching high and low for Julia, to no avail. Kim is raising your son alone and he's starting to ask about you. It won't be long before she's forced to tell him that Daddy is out trying to save a girl, but apparently he sucks at it. With great regret, you decide to come home as a failure and raise your son the best that you can.

You don't want to come home empty-handed, so when you get back to your town you stop into the supermarket near Kim's house to pick up some groceries and a few sweets for your boy. It's quite a shock when you find Julia standing in the condiments aisle. She's got a man by her side, and a baby in her cart.

"This is Leon, my husband," she says.

Leon says hi.

"We've spoken before," you say. You recognize his voice as the voice that called you about the ransom five years earlier. They take you to the snack counter and buy you a Superpretzel to eat while they explain everything.

It turns out that Leon was Julia's ex-boyfriend whom she broke up with right before seeing you. He got pretty crazy with jealousy, and on a whim he bought a ski mask and rented a van and ended up kidnapping her at the end of your first date together.

"Once we were alone," Julia says, "he revealed who he was and I guess the excitement kind of reignited the spark. So we decided to give it another go. Except he'd already committed a felony by kidnapping me. We couldn't exactly just explain it all to you and hope you'd be cool with it."

"So we left town and laid low," Leon says.

"Just like that? You just went on the lam?" you ask.

"We wanted to be together," Julia says. "Sometimes you just have to make a decision in the moment and do what you can later to make sure it was the right one."

"We had little Leona here while we were away," Leon says. "After a few years we came back here because we decided this is a pretty good place to raise a family."

"I bet it is," you agree. You accept their apologies and

then excuse yourself so you can race to Kim's house. She opens the door with hope in her eyes.

You smile at the mother of your firstborn and you say, "Found her!" Then you go inside to be a father to your son.

THE END

Wedding Day at the Safe House

The kidnappers were nice enough to wear white hoods for the occasion. Julia and Reggie spent several days making paper carnations out of tissues and napkins, and they are festooned throughout the basement, making it all look very festive. Chet and Reggie are seated on the bed, and Marcus stands before you as the officiant. Sam didn't feel like coming downstairs. You can hear the TV through the ceiling. It sounds like he's watching a *Friends* rerun.

"I understand the bride and groom have written their own vows," Marcus says through his hood.

You read yours first:

> *It couldn't be more fitting to have these men here today to witness us enter this union, since they are the men who gave us no choice but to be together. Leading up to today, I've had to ask myself, am I only marrying you because I have not been in contact with any other woman in four years? Perhaps. But if you ask any free man in love, he'll tell you that there are no other women, except for the woman with whom he is in love.*
>
> *Julia, I may not be free, but I have found freedom in your arms.*

Julia is in tears when you finish. She unfolds her piece of paper and begins to read:

> *Is our love able to survive only because we are being held captive at gunpoint? Maybe. But are*

there not also men and women in the free world whose love can only survive because they are wealthy, or because they are both Presbyterians, or because they live in California?

A very small part of me is glad that I was kidnapped, because it was the kidnapping that brought us closer together. I may never know whether we would have stayed together if we had remained free, and I'm glad I don't have to find out. A kidnapping brought us together, but a rescue will never tear us apart.

When the two of you kiss, a loud explosion is heard upstairs. The kidnappers race out the door and you and Julia lie on the ground listening to lots of shouting and gunfire. When it's quiet, footsteps are heard on the stairs and a squad of policemen in tactical gear enter the basement and lead you to safety.

If you want to remain married to each other in the outside world, go to page 155.

If you want to split up immediately, go to page 7.

Worst. Booty Call. Ever.

At around 11:40 you get bored waiting for the kidnappers to call, so you dial your ex-girlfriend Kim to try and make sure you're the last person she talks to before bed. You're glad to be out of the relationship, but you don't want her to move on with her life, either.

"This is the fifth night this week," she says groggily. She was asleep. "You know this doesn't work, right? I'm not going to dream about you just because you're the last person I speak to before I fall asleep." Kim's getting a masters in psychology. She spent eight years after college trying to get steady work as a theatrical costume designer and temping to pay the rent, but she got sick of being poor and listening to actors whine about chafing.

"This isn't like when I called because I saw that shooting star or when I couldn't find my Veruca Salt CD," you say. "I really have something to tell you this time. I've had a big day."

You tell her about the kidnapping and about Lenny coming back from the dead to convince you to give up on acting. Kim asks if you were seeing Julia before you and she broke up. She finds it hard to believe that you went on one date and you're already rescuing her from kidnappers and giving up on your dreams for her.

"She's from out of town," you say. "And Lenny came back from the dead. He was still fifteen and still wet and nude. How could I not do what he says?"

"I don't want you to call me anymore," Kim says. "This is hurting me. I need us to cut off all communication."

You hear a call-waiting beep but you don't answer because you don't want to hang up on Kim. Her declaration has sent you into a panic that you never would have predicted. You try to convince her that the two of you can stay friends and you'll respect her boundaries, but she interrupts you.

"It's twelve oh two," she says. "Wasn't the kidnapper supposed to call at midnight?"

Another call-waiting comes in.

"You have to take that. That girl could die," Kim says. Then she hangs up.

Your stomach is in knots when you click over to the other line.

"Hey, it's Chet," you hear. "What the fuck?"

"Chet?"

"The kidnapper, idiot. I called at midnight but you didn't answer."

"The kidnapper?"

Chet sounds annoyed. "Yes. The kidnapper. What, did you fucking forget?"

"I just didn't think you'd offer your name like that," you say. "Since kidnapping is illegal and all."

Chet takes a second. "Maybe it's a fake name."

"Is it?"

"Look, do you have the money or are we gonna have to kill your girlfriend?"

"She's not my girlfriend," you say. "Yes, I have the money. Where should I bring it?"

Chet says, "Tomorrow at noon. The Ten-K Marathon for Breast Cancer Research. The finish line. And remember, no police. I repeat, do not call the police."

If you want to call the police and let them handle it so that you can go to Kim and convince her to keep you in her life, even though you don't want to get back together or anything, you just don't want to try to live without her yet, go to page 70.

If you want to show up at the finish line tomorrow, go to page 22.

Insufficient Funds

Mr. Hancock, the bank manager, looks at your check, then at you. "I can't cash this," he says. "I received a phone call from your father's divorce lawyer ordering me to cancel the check. Apparently your mother alerted her divorce lawyer of this payment, and he threatened to accuse your father of trying to liquidate his assets before a judgment could be entered in their divorce."

You go cold. "They're going to kill her. What am I supposed to do?"

Mr. Hancock leans in close to you. He takes your hand. "Any fool can pay a thug and have his love handed back to him as if he were purchasing gum from a drugstore. But use your cunning, your strength, and any weapons you can get your hands on, and this woman will know what you are made of, and what she means to you."

"But I already told them I'd pay," you say. "They're waiting for me."

"Bluff," Mr. Hancock says.

"I can't," you say. "It won't work."

Mr. Hancock's grip on your hand tightens. "Thugs traffic in deceit and cowardice. Pay them in kind. Bluff. GO NOW!" he shouts.

Emboldened by Mr. Hancock's words, you go back to the finish line and tell Chet that his money's on the way, it's just going to take a few days for the funds to clear in your dad's account.

"But don't worry," you say. "He's got lots of money. He's loaded."

"Great," Chet says. "Then we'll kidnap you, too, and we'll get even more out of him."

A black hood is yanked down over your head and you hear the squeal of tires. Many hands grab you and throw you into the back of a van. When they finally take the hood off your head, you are in the basement of a safe house with Julia.

If you want to try to escape, go to page 96.

If you want to just chill out and wait for your dad to come around and pay the ransom or for the police to burst in or something like that, go to page 31.

You Are the Face of America's Decline

When you hang up with Chet, you immediately call the police and tell them everything you know about the kidnapping. You give them the drop location and the time, and you warn that the kidnappers have made several threats on Julia's life. Then you warn them that you were told not to involve the police, and that they'll kill Julia if they see any policemen. "So, try to hide or something. Maybe use snipers," you say.

You hear silence on the other end. Then, "What's it like to be you?"

"Sorry?" you say.

"You know, most of the time," the policeman says. "When someone gets told by a kidnapper not to involve the police, they try to keep the police out of it. Even though they know that the police would handle the situation better than them, they worry that disobeying the kidnappers' orders will be like pulling the trigger on their loved one. But you didn't worry about that, did you? You just called us right up."

"It's just a really weird situation," you say. "I don't even know this girl. And there's this thing with my ex-girlfriend that's got me really confused."

"I just wanna know what it's like," the policeman says. "To be conscienceless. Can't be bothered. Always on the lookout for the nearest exit sign in case anyone starts to expect anything of you."

You want more than anything to hang up the phone, but then you won't be sure if he'll follow through on rescuing Julia, and you'd be left to handle things yourself.

"Must be lonely," the policeman says.

You keep quiet. You've faced this kind of questioning in the past—most recently, during your breakup with Kim.

"Is it lonely?" he asks.

"It is," you say.

"Exhausting, too, I'd imagine," the cop continues. "It must take a lot of running around to keep from ever being pinned down."

"I get tired," you admit. "With nothing to show for it. When I look at how little I've accomplished, it's hard not to be upset with myself."

You hear the policeman scribbling.

"Are you writing this down?" you ask.

"You interest me," the cop says. "Working this job, I get to wondering sometimes whether it's the criminals who are ruining everything, or the citizens who just won't lift a finger to keep it all from crumbling down. When this is all over I'd really like to pick your brain. See what makes a man turn out like you."

You tell the policeman that'd be fine and you wish him luck on saving Julia, hoping that will be the end of it.

"We could use your help," the cop says. "Seeing as you're the one they've been contacting. You're not just going to hang up and let us take care of this on our own, are you? Come on, you wanna take a crack at doing what's right?"

If you want to take a crack at doing what's right and help the police, go to page 37.

If you wanna just let the police handle it so that you can go see Kim, even though it will pretty much guarantee Julia's gonna die, go to page 163.

Tell Your Dad His Little Boy
Is All Growed Up

Inside the factory, your dad and Julia sit side by side at the far end of the dilapidated space. They are both bound and gagged. There are four kidnappers total. Three of them aim their guns at your dad and at Julia. One stands empty-handed, waiting for you as you approach.

"You can call me Chet," he says when you reach him. "Though that's not necessarily my real name."

"Sorry about my dad sneaking up on you, Chet," you say. "I told him you just wanted us to deliver the cash, but he never listens to me."

Chet says, "Well, we've got him bound and gagged. He'll listen to you now if you got anything you want to say."

The kidnappers gather to count the money. You go and kneel next to your dad so you can speak into his ear.

"Dad, it's me, your son," you say, even though he can see you. "I'm thirty-three now, Dad. Can you believe it? Your little boy's a thirty-three-year-old man. I know I don't really act like one, but maybe it's time for me to start. I know you just want to protect me, but I want to make you proud. How can I do that if you're always swooping in to make my decisions for me? You need to trust me more, Dad. I know you might be afraid that I won't need you anymore, but you don't have to worry. I'll always be your son. Trust me."

The kidnappers finish counting the money. Chet leans toward you and whispers, "That was very strong. Very honest."

You stand up. "Thanks," you say.

"Now which one do we kill?" Chet asks.

He claims that $50,000 only buys you one life. Now that there are two, someone has to die.

"Your father or your girlfriend? Which one do we kill?"

If you want to tell them to kill your dad, go to page 45.

If you want to tell them to kill Julia, go to page 146.

A Rescue Composed Entirely of Holograms

First they have you Star-69 the kidnapper's phone number and tell him that you want to change the drop spot to the old abandoned ketchup factory on the outskirts of town, tomorrow at midnight. The kidnapper says okay.

"Wait a minute," Cortez says. "Why'd he agree so easily? I smell a trap."

To protect you from the trap that Officer Cortez smells, he decides to film a hologram of you bringing the money into the factory. It is a painstakingly detailed process that keeps you up all night, especially since Officer Frank has a tendency to half-ass the lighting design. But they manage to get a passable cut together in time.

The kidnapper must have smelled a trap, too, so he also decided to film a hologram of himself holding Julia captive inside the factory. Though both parties thought they were outsmarting each other, at midnight the only thing that happens is a couple of light-projected images say and do a bunch of crap that makes no sense at all.

The hologram of the kidnapper stands at the far end of the factory aiming a gun at a hologram of Julia. The hologram of you enters the factory with your hands up, holding the briefcase over your head. You walk very slowly.

"Put your hands up and walk very slowly," the kidnapper's hologram shouts.

Your hologram shouts, "How do I know Julia is alive?"

The hologram of Julia, which is standing in plain sight in

front of your hologram, shouts, "Don't believe him, it's a trap!"

The kidnapper's hologram smacks Julia's hologram on the head. His hologram yells, "If you two try to get smart again you'll see her brains all over this floor! Now put the case on the ground and kick it to me!"

Your hologram shouts, "Show me the girl or the deal's off!"

Though your hologram is still holding the briefcase, another hologram of a briefcase, which the kidnapper filmed, suddenly slides across the floor toward the kidnapper. He bends down and opens the case and starts counting the money.

"I mean it," your hologram says. "Produce the girl or you don't get the money!"

The kidnapper's hologram checks a few packs of bills for markings. "Looks like it's all here," he says.

Your hologram says, "I'm not kidding. I'll toss the money into the river! Show me the girl!"

The kidnapper's hologram sets the hologram of Julia free. He says, "Pleasure doing business with ya!" The hologram of Julia runs joyfully toward your hologram, but ends up stopping six feet to the left of your hologram. Julia's hologram is crying and making out with nothing while yours shouts, "That's it! Deal's off!" That's when a hologram of fifty federal agents swarms through the windows and opens fire. After a few minutes and a whole lot of noise, the factory goes dark and the raccoons that live there continue in their peaceful foraging.

Later, the real you stands outside the factory with the real Officer Cortez and the rest of the real police.

"You're lucky I thought to make a hologram of you," Office Cortez says. "I'm extremely cunning."

"One thing I don't get, Officer Cortez," you say. "Filming my hologram took hours and it was a terribly involved and precise endeavor. If Julia was in the kidnapper's hologram and saying all of those things, she had to have been filmed doing what the kidnapper told her to do. She must have cooperated."

"Hell, yes," Officer Cortez says. "That took a lot of rehearsal, too. Quality stuff."

"Does this mean . . . ?"

Officer Cortez puts a hand on your shoulder. "I'm afraid it's not uncommon for a kidnap victim to take a shine to her captor. Looks like your girlfriend might be one of the bad guys now."

If you want to find out that Julia was brainwashed into falling in love with her kidnapper, go to page 79.

If you want to find out that Julia was forced into mastering the art of stereo-component sales, go to page 110.

Your Dad Is a Miserable Excuse for a Hero

You have no idea how relieved your dad is that you finally decided to let him take care of the situation for you. It's not just that he's afraid of his baby leaving the nest. He's also afraid that if you stop seeing him as your life preserver, you might finally have the chance to take an objective evaluation of what sort of man he turned out to be, the man you're probably doomed to become as well. He'd rather postpone that day for as long as he can. He can already see himself in you, and that disgusts him. Like any father, he always wanted better for his son, and if he can't have that, he'd rather you not find out what's in store until it's too late.

"Open up the glove compartment and hand me that gun," he says. You never knew he had a gun. "I'm gonna go around back and see if I can't get some idea of what they're up to in there."

"But they just want us to deliver the money," you say.

"I just want to get a look at what their position is," he says. Then he chuckles and musses your hair. "Don't worry, kiddo. Daddy's gonna make it all better."

Your dad runs off toward the rear of the factory and is instantly captured. The kidnappers start shouting at you to come in and bring the money or they're going to kill both your dad and Julia.

If you want to go into the factory with the money, go to page 73.

If you want to just sit there in the car, go to page 48.

She'll Learn to Love You

A voice shouts through Officer Cortez's walkie-talkie. "Cortez, we got a visual on the girl."

They find Julia tied up behind the factory. When they remove the gag from her mouth, she is crying and screaming for her kidnapper, who left her behind and took off when he saw that the police had set a trap.

The police question her for a few weeks, but she gives them nothing to help catch him. You and Julia start dating again, trying to pick up where you left off. It's difficult, because the kidnapper brainwashed her into thinking he's the tops and she can't stop saying things like "My captor would have picked a nicer restaurant" and "That totally reminds me of something far more hilarious and witty that my captor once said. . . ."

You finally tell her that you can't go on seeing her if she insists on unconditionally and irrationally worshipping the existence of the man from whom you helped rescue her. She says that she really wants to try and make it work with you, so she consents to deprogramming.

The deprogrammers work with her night and day, trying to turn the idea of her kidnapper into a negative stimulus. They show her a photo of her kidnapper immediately followed by giving her an electric shock or pouring a gallon of oil down her throat. You paid extra to have them associate you with positive stimuli, and so every once in a while they'll show her a photo of you accompanied by the smell of homemade cookies or a sip from a really well-made frozen margarita.

After thirty days held captive, you go to the deprogramming center (you get there through a secret panel in the mop closet of a Chili's) and wait for Julia to come out and be your girlfriend. The deprogrammers escort her into the waiting room. She's very shaken, but still very pretty despite some notable hair loss. When she sees you, she smiles.

"I love you because you're the good things," Julia says.

"You're the good things, too," you tell her.

"And you're not the bad things," she says. "The shocks and the oil. You're not shocks and oil."

After several weeks of Julia loving you with all the strength of someone who believes you are the direct opposite of electric shock aversion therapy and the taste of fossil fuel, you start to feel like the relationship is a little uneven. So you go back to the deprogramming center and ask them to program you to associate Julia with positive stimuli as well. "Our relationship isn't on the level. I want to feel what she feels," you tell them. "I want to see her as the opposite of pain."

After a month of reprogramming, your feelings for Julia go from potentially loving to the belief that she is a soft, warm, and bulletproof and flame-retardant blanket under which no one can ever hurt you. You stay together forever, each of you loving the other the way a child loves its mother. It gets difficult to lead your lives and pursue careers because any time you're apart you both just fall to the ground shrieking with the belief that the bad things are coming. So you open up a coffee shop together, furnish it with mismatched and uncomfortable thrift-store chairs, and you live happily ever after in the constant presence of the only thing that makes you both feel safe: each other.

THE END

Reach into the Mirror and Touch Yourself

You go out and buy some posterboard, on which you write in magic marker: MIDNIGHT—PARKING LOT BEHIND THE SAFE-WAY. $50,000.

You hold the posterboard up over your head and you start walking around your apartment, standing in the middle of the floor and spinning in a circle so that your sign is aimed at every possible wall and surface where a camera might be hidden. Then you lay the sign faceup on your bed, which is the one place where you know the camera can record you.

At midnight, you stand in the middle of the parking lot behind the Safeway with your briefcase full of cash. A black Lexus pulls up to you and a man in a black hood steps out of the car.

"I said wait for my call!" he says. "Do you know how far away my safe house is from here? Are you trying to get her killed?"

"Get who killed?" you say. "I just want more DVDs. I know you're the guy who's been watching me in my apartment. That's fine. I just want to buy the DVDs of me masturbating. The way it will work is, each day I'll masturbate to the last DVD of me masturbating that you sent me. You'll tape that, and the next day you'll send me the next level. I'll give you fifty thousand dollars."

The man is stunned. "That fifty thousand dollars was ransom money. To save Julia."

"How do you know about that?"

The man in the hood explains that he is a kidnapper for hire and he works for a very powerful man who is obsessed with you. "He sent you that DVD to let you know that there is a mad genius who has been audience to your every private moment for many years now. I am only in his employ and I do not know his intentions, but I know he has no interest in helping you to masturbate until you collapse in on yourself."

"What if I used the money for Julia's ransom?" you ask. "Then I pay you separately to make those DVDs of me masturbating to myself masturbating. How much would that cost me?"

Exhausted, he says, "He won't record you masturbating. Now do you want to save the girl or not?"

You're about to burst into tears. "But how do I get a recording of me masturbating to myself?!"

The man in the hood summons all the patience he has left and suggests that you purchase a video camera and set it so that you and your TV are in the frame. You can then make the recordings on your own ad infinitum until the first image of you masturbating is nothing more than a single flickering pixel.

"Now give me the money," he says.

You hand him the briefcase. The kidnapper opens the rear door of his Lexus and out steps Julia.

"This isn't over! My employer has very big plans for you," the man tells you. To Julia he whispers, "Play the field." Then he speeds off into the night.

Julia thanks you and you rush to get her home. The

next morning, you race to Best Buy and purchase a video camera and numerous tapes and you embark on your great and ecstatic journey inward. Whoever's watching you is going to get quite an eyeful from now on!

THE END

Just Married!

You tell Reggie you think he's bluffing, and you go through with the wedding, and it's magical. Immediately after the ceremony, Chet gives you your wedding present.

"You're released!" he shouts.

They blindfold you and drive you out to a highway and set you free to forge ahead as husband and wife, suddenly released back into society. You divorce within minutes.

THE END

Meet the Guy Your Mom Actually Gave a Shit About

Now that your dad likes you, you feel indestructible. So you start driving recklessly and you immediately crash his car into a ditch. You run to the nearest house to try to get help.

Through the window you spy an old man sitting in his living room, caressing a picture frame. You knock on his door and tell him that a girl's been kidnapped and you need a ride to the ransom drop. "I'm trying to prove to my dad that I am deserving of his pride. Please don't let me blow this, mister!"

The old man stares at you with his mouth agape. "Those eyes," he says. Then he drops the picture frame and it shatters on the ground. Under the shards of glass you see that it is a picture of your mother when she was eighteen. The old man invites you in.

"I used to love to dress your mother," he says. His name is Herbert and he was the costume designer at the community theater where your mother acted for a few years when she was young. "Those curves and contours were my inspiration for every piece I would design. I couldn't wait to drape my clothes over her shoulders and watch the garment take form over those beautiful breasts and those hips—oh, your mother's hips."

Herbert was so enamored with your mother's body that he inevitably made the mistake of trying to get inside it. But the bond between your mother and Herbert was born from the act of artistic creation. After they had sex, it was as if his muse had been dragged down to earth and he could no longer create.

"I felt sabotaged," Herbert said. "And yet I loved her. So I did what so many men did back then when they felt baffled by love. I enlisted to go and fight in Korea."

By the time the Korean conflict had ended, your mother had already left town to pursue acting in New York City, where she would later meet your father.

"But I never stopped loving her. And I've never loved anyone quite so strongly," Herbert says.

It's hard to believe your mother could ever have been party to the sort of love Herbert describes. You feel sad for all she might have missed, but you also feel defensive of your father in light of your newfound bond with him.

"Now then, you need my car," Herbert says. "I'll tell you what. Put me in contact with your mother, give us the chance to reclaim that love we so carelessly threw away, and I'll give you the keys."

Putting Herbert in contact with your mom would be a direct betrayal of your father. But without that car, you'll never make it to the ransom drop in time, and you will prove to your father that his pride in you was misplaced.

"Hurry, son," Herbert says, placing his withered hand over yours. "There isn't much time."

If you want to deliver your mother to Herbert so you can get the car, go to page 93.

If you want to defend your father's honor and tell Herbert you'll find another car, go to page 44.

Rescuing for Two

When you step outside the building, you're feeling proud of yourself for having told Danny to keep his check. Suddenly, a blue Honda Accord comes careening around the corner with Kim behind the wheel.

"I'm pregnant," she says. "It's yours. I don't know if I want to keep it or not, but if I do, you don't have to be involved. The only thing you have to do is make sure you save this girl from those kidnappers. You can't flake out on this like you do with everything else and leave me to one day tell my baby that his daddy let a girl die because he was too self-absorbed to lift a finger for her."

"So that means if you choose to abort, I don't have to rescue the girl, right?"

"So what?" Kim says. "It's four forty-five. You only have until midnight to save that girl, and I'm not going to decide to abort before midnight."

You start arguing that it's your baby, too, and she shouldn't have the final say in whether or not it gets aborted within the next seven hours and fifteen minutes.

"I'm the father!" you shout. "If I think the baby should be aborted before midnight tonight, it should count for something."

Kim tells you that the abortion clinic closes in fifteen minutes and it'd be next to impossible to get there in time, so you're just going to have to conduct yourself as if you're going to be a father.

"What sort of man do you want your baby's father to be?" she asks.

If you want to race to the abortion clinic to try to get your baby aborted before five, go to page 28.

If you want to embrace your impending fatherhood and use that little life as an inspiration for you to be the bravest and noblest man that you can be, go to page 59.

Just Say No to Anonymous Roadside Humping

"I can't," **you** say. "I'm . . ."

"You're making your daddy proud," she says. "I can't blame you. If I thought I could make someone proud of me I doubt I'd be wasting my time looking for strangers to touch me on a bench."

You start to go. The woman in the lycra top says, "Wait."

You turn.

"Will you hold my hand?" she asks. "I'm just so cold."

She holds her hand out and you take it in yours. It really is cold.

"Thank you," she says. "That helped."

You go back to your car and continue to the ransom drop, where you exchange the ransom money for Julia's life.

When she gets in the car, you hold her close to you. "I don't know where this is going between you and me," you say to her. "I don't know if we're even going to have a second date. But if we do keep seeing each other and we end up getting married and having kids, we have to be sure to let those kids know we're proud of them."

"Of course we would. Think I want my kids to go looking for sex at highway rest stops?" Julia laughs. Then she puts her hands on your cheeks. "My God, you're shivering."

You smile and you kiss her once on the lips. Then you

take her home and make plans for a drink with her later in the week. Someplace nice and indoors.

THE END

Herbert Hearts Your Mom

Herbert won't let you take the car until he lays eyes on your mom again, so you call her and convince her to come to his house. "I'll be right there," she pants when you tell her who you're with. Her excitement at the prospect of reuniting with her long-lost lover makes you feel all the worse for your Dad.

The minute she walks through the door Herbert's got a tape measure around her bust and he starts writing down measurements to make her a new gown. You leave Herbert to celebrate your mother's hips and contours in beautiful draping fabric and you take his car to the abandoned ketchup factory where you exchange the ransom money for Julia's life. It was surprisingly easy.

You bring Julia home after the rescue to show her off to your Dad. He's got his head in his hands and he doesn't bother to look up at her when she says hello.

"She's gone," your dad says. You see a note in his hands. You know what it says without him having to tell you.

You try to cheer him up by showing him what a great job you did. "Look, Dad," you say, spinning Julia around in the living room. "Not a scratch on her."

Your dad looks up now. He takes in the sight of Julia spinning in the middle of his living room. "I'm proud of you, son. You did it all by yourself," he says. "Looks like nobody needs me."

He lets his head drop again into the hand that holds your mom's note. "I always knew she had a love in her past," your dad says. "After all these years, I thought she was over it."

He gets up from the couch and goes to his bedroom. "If you know it's right," he says while walking away, "never let each other go. Otherwise, you never know who you'll hurt down the line." Then he shuts his bedroom door and begins his life alone.

Julia wants to celebrate her new freedom but you tell her you're too worn out and you take her home. In the span of one day, you saved a girl's life, sent your mother back into the arms of the only man she ever really loved, and broke your father's heart. You could use a rest.

THE END

Use Your Sexy Body

You're terrified of being released back into the free world, where you'll be expected to pursue a career and try to achieve something remotely memorable before you die. You'd prefer to stay in the basement for as long as possible. So you promise Reggie that he can do whatever he wants to you, as long as he makes sure that you don't get released.

"I won't call off the wedding," you say. "I can't hurt Julia. But you can have me in secret."

Reggie agrees to your terms. You go through with the wedding and it is magical. Afterward, Reggie comes into the basement every night at around seven while Julia showers, and he does stuff to you. And you don't hear any more talk about a possible release.

It isn't until months later that you find out Reggie lied about the release. Chet comes down with Reggie to make him apologize.

"I just wanted you so," Reggie explains.

"We wouldn't have released you until we got the money," Chet says. "We're kidnappers, not quitters. But we're not rapists, either. I can't have that kind of thing happening to people in my captivity. I have to let you go."

So they blindfold you and Julia and drive you out to a highway and set you both free to forge ahead as husband and wife. You divorce within minutes.

THE END

Never Join a Sex Club That Would Have Your Grandfather as a Member

You and Julia take one look at each other and immediately start searching the basement for a way out. It looks to be completely impenetrable, and you give up after not too long and sit on the bed that's there.

In the silence, Julia asks, "What was that?"

You hear it, too. It's barely audible—a low, long hum coming from the floor. It might be just an electrical box or a heating pipe deep underground, except the hum changes octaves.

It's human.

The two of you frantically rip up the carpet from the floor and you start searching around the floorboards with your hands until you locate a wider crack. You follow the crack and find that it forms a rectangle. It's definitely hollow underneath.

"It's a door," Julia says, watching you.

You try to dig your fingernails into the crack but you don't feel any give.

"There must be some sort of secret lever in here," you say.

You and Julia walk around the room tugging and yanking at everything that's attached to the wall until she finally lifts a framed print of a Klimt painting off the wall and the door in the floor creaks up and open.

You bend over it to see a steep stone staircase leading down into the darkness. The humming echoes up from whatever's down there. Together you descend dozens of steps before you see light again—candlelight, illuminating a vast and ornate chamber. The humming is so loud, there must be hundreds of people down there.

You reach a stone balcony overlooking the center of the chamber. Below you are the people you heard. They are gathered in circles. Groups of them are having sex in the circles while the rest watch and hum from the perimeters. They wear silver cloaks, some with designs painted in glitter on the back. The youngest of them can't be a day under fifty, and many of them are well into their golden years. Occasionally, whether they climax or not, the aged couple in the center of each circle will stop having sex and change partners, pulling the humming, dottering onlookers into the center to pick up where they left off. When they slip into their cloaks and cover up their ruined, sagging flesh, you whisper a little thank-you to God, which you follow with a curse against him when you catch sight of another couple that has dropped their cloaks to the ground.

You and Julia are completely bewildered and not just a little nauseous. Before you have to look at too many of them, you shout, "Who are you people!"

The humming stops, as does the sex, and everyone turns to look up at you and Julia. The crowd erupts with shouts of "Intruder!" and "Destroy the temple!" and "Crap, I was close!" Then a man emerges from the center of the mass. He slips on a robe to cover his nakedness (for which you are infinitely grateful) before answering your question.

"We are all disciples of the Order of the Rune. You have discovered us in the middle of our harvest celebration," he says. "We gather here at the turn of the seasons to commingle our spirits."

"Oh," you say. "So it's like an orgy?"

"All of us are married," he says. "Man to woman and woman to man, each marriage married to the next. It is here, deep in the earth at the turn of the seasons, that our vast union is consummated."

Julia says, "So you're swingers?"

The man clears his throat. "Disciples of the Order of the Rune," he repeats sternly. "And who the hell are you?"

"We've been kidnapped," you say. "We were locked in the basement at the top of the steps. We need to find a way out."

"There have been built many paths of entrance and exit, and we'd be happy to lead you to safety, but no one may enter this temple unless they have also taken a marriage vow to be honorable and loving to his and her fellow disciples."

"You mean," Julia says, "we have to marry you?"

"We would welcome you with love. As you can see, we are all of us well beyond our fruitful years and we are in need of brides and bridegrooms who are a bit more vibrant and, well, toned."

You and Julia note the excited eyes and hungry smiles on the faces of the other congregants. You look to Julia and she is terrified. She shakes her head.

"I'm sorry," you say. "We're just not ready to get married right now."

The disciples are crestfallen. You feel as if you've just broken up with the whole room.

"That is unfortunate," the bearded man says. "Taze them!"

Several elderly men with silver cloaks hiding their soft-ons come out of the shadows and taze you. Paralyzed with electric shock, you're dragged down to the floor and placed on two altars.

"I am sorry," the bearded man says. "This temple houses our marital bond. When an outsider intrudes upon that bond, especially during consummation, they must either enter into the bond or be sacrificed."

"Look, we won't tell anyone about your orgy," you shout.

"I am sorry," the bearded man says. "Join our marriage, or die."

Without any discussion, you and Julia agree to being sacrificed rather than marrying into an elderly sex cult. Unfortunately, they won't kill you until after they are finished with their orgy, and no matter how much you beg, they refuse to give you blindfolds. You do your best to close your eyes against the sight of so much spotted skin, but it's no use. To speed up your end, you and Julia slam your heads into the concrete underneath you until your skulls have cracked.

Once the orgy has ended, they first have to remove the corpses of those orgy participants who died of natural causes (nine dead, a new record). Finally, the bearded man returns to the two of you to find that you've managed to take your own lives.

"If only they were able to accept the love we have to give," he says to his henchmen. "Perhaps we could have made them happy enough to go on."

The bearded men and his henchmen fondle your still

bodies until you go cold, then you are added to the pile of dead to be burned. At the next orgy, just before the minutes are read, you and the other dead will be thanked for the joy you gave while alive.

THE END

A Little "You Time"

You spend the day making no effort whatsoever to gather the fifty thousand dollars. You think about Kim. You destroyed your relationship with Kim, kicked it in the knees at every turn. And this morning, you got to crawl inside the wreckage and draw from it bliss. You think about the sex you just had and why it was so much better than the sex you used to have when you were together. You know the thrill of the forbidden added some of the kick. But there was something perverse about it, too.

What the fuck is wrong with me? you think. *Who am I to save that girl? If she lives through the kidnapping I'll just be the one to end up hurting her. Fuck this.*

You rip the phone cord from the wall and carry the phone into the kitchen to get your bottle of Maker's Mark. Back in your chair, you begin drinking quietly while staring at the wall in front of you. You realize the phone is still in your hand. You take another sip from the bottle, and then you fling the phone across the room to crash into pieces against the wall.

THE END

They Said No Cops!

They take you down to the police station and pump you for more details while they plan their assault on the kidnappers. You end up sleeping on a couch in one of the offices and you wake up the next day at 2 P.M.

You wander out to find Officer Cortez at his desk with his head in his hands.

"Where's Officer Frank?" you ask.

Cortez gives you a look of surprise, as if he'd forgotten you were still around. He says, "Dead. Frank's dead." Then he puts his head back in his hands.

"Where's Julia?" you ask.

Officer Cortez doesn't answer. You look down and notice that you're standing in your tube socks, which feels very strange considering the rising tide of panic that's sweeping over you.

"Is Julia dead?"

Cortez nods. "They dumped her body not long after."

"What happened?"

He looks up and says, "Frank botched the raid on the site. He called their bluff, but he moved too soon and the kidnappers took off with the girl. Frank couldn't handle it. He grabbed a squad car, drove to the waterfront, and shot himself in the head with his service revolver."

You look down at your socks again. You want more than anything for Cortez to put his head in his hands so you can walk back into the office and put on your shoes. But Cortez walks over to you and puts his hand on your shoulder. One of his shoes lands on the empty toe of the sock that is dangling off of your foot like a rabbit's ear. You're pinned.

"Don't blame yourself for my partner's death," he says. "He wanted this too much. He wasn't doing his job out there. He was trying to settle a score with himself, but he was playing with someone else's life. He couldn't go on living with the knowledge that he'd allowed two innocent people to die. It's his fault, not yours. Do you believe that?"

You nod.

"Julia's death is your fault, though. That's totally on you."

"But how was I supposed to save her!" you whine.

"Hell if I know. But you could have started by listening to the kidnappers and not telling the cops."

"But I took a crack at doing what's right!" you say.

"Yeah, after you involved the police. But the police weren't supposed to be involved, were they?"

"Why are you doing this?" you ask.

Officer Cortez says, "I am not going to shoulder this burden for you. I am not going to end up like my partner. I tried to do my job and it didn't work. Too bad. But that girl died because you tried to weasel out of your responsibility. Understand?"

"But—"

"Understand!" Cortez barks. You try to pull your sock out from under his shoe but it won't budge.

"It's on me," you say. "It's my fault."

Cortez lifts his foot off of your sock and walks back to his desk.

"I'm sorry," you say.

Cortez throws his hands up in the air. You put your shoes back on and leave the station to head back home.

THE END

Kill Everyone in Sight, Then Tell Julia Not to See This as Some Kind of Big Commitment

You quit your job and go home to wait for the kidnapper to call. At midnight, the phone rings.

"Do you have the money?"

"Yeah," you say.

"Bring it to the old abandoned ketchup factory on the edge of town at noon tomorrow," the voice says.

You hang up, then say aloud, "If they think they're getting one red cent out of me, they've got another thing coming." Then you laugh a sinister laugh.

The next morning, you use your credit card to buy guns and bombs and some printer cartridges (yours have been empty for weeks). You go to the ketchup factory and shoot everyone except Julia. One guy gets to his car and drives off, so you throw a bomb at the car and blow it up.

When you limp away from the carnage with Julia in your arms, you say, "You know this doesn't mean anything. I'm still getting over somebody, and—"

Julia interrupts you with a kiss on your lips. "Thank you," she says. Then she walks away to hail a cab.

As she's getting into a cab, you shout, "Hey, can I call ya?"

She smiles and shouts back, "You better!" Then she slams the door of the cab and heads home safe and sound.

THE END

Wax On, Wax Off

Now that you are a man in love, Ray the Real Rain takes you into the forest, makes you strip naked, and leaves you there for five days. "You have something to live for now," he says. "You'll stay alive."

He's right. Guided by the wisdom of your love, you quickly find shelter in a reindeer's carcass. After five days, Ray the Real Rain returns to the forest and teaches you to embrace your love and convert it into merciless fury.

"The vigilante both defends justice and uses the spirit of justice as his strength," he says. "Likewise, the love vigilante acts in defense of his love, while at the same time using the strength of his love to unleash his vengeance upon all those who try to keep him and his beloved apart. Your love is the bullets in your gun, the sheen on your blade, the 'don't-even-try-it' scowl on your lips."

Rain teaches you to use those butterflies in your stomach to help you kill silently and without remorse. By remembering how Julia laughed at a funny thing you said on your date, you find you have the nerve to dig your fingers into a foe's throat and remove his voicebox with one mean tug. When you imagine Julia's touch upon your hand, you have the strength to end a man's life with a single punch to his heart. The love flowing from your heart to your fingertips steadies your hand when firing assault rifles or releasing throwing stars. And though this should only be used when doing battle with five men or more, if you imagine a teardrop on Julia's cheek, the bloody mess you will leave in your wake will cause area residents to pour Clorox into their trash cans because they'll think there are bears in the area.

"Everything's in perfect focus," you say to Ray the Real Rain on one of your breaks. "I know who I am. I know what I'm meant to do."

"Ain't love grand," Rain says.

After your final lesson, in which Rain teaches you how to use your love to crack safes, he says, "Student, you are ready. Go and unleash your love upon the world."

If you want to use the power of love for good,
go to page 119.

If you want to use the power of love for evil,
go to page 148.

Julia Sells Speakers and Shit Like That Now

Several years after giving up the hunt for Julia, you decide it's time you bought yourself a bitchin' new stereo-component system, one that has a tweeter. You go down to Irving's Speaker Kingdom to find out just how hard you can rock your neighbors' world by spending the entirety of your savings ($575).

When you arrive at Irving's Speaker Kingdom, you are assigned a lady speaker salesperson, which bugs you because you like it when guy speaker salesmen tell you how easily a particular speaker will make girls in your apartment get nude, and you bet the lady speaker salesperson will be much more proper about the whole exchange. You feel better, though, when the lady speaker salesperson greets you, because she's a superhot lady and she looks and sounds just like Julia, except this lady has weird blond hair that doesn't seem to match the rest of her face. You think about Julia every day, and it's nice to talk to someone who reminds you of her.

"I understand you're finally ready to rock your world appropriately," the lady speaker salesperson says. "You've come to the right place. Here at Irving's Speaker Kingdom, the speaker is king, and the king has decreed that music must be set free."

"That rocks," you say.

"Now you're rocking," the lady speaker salesperson says. "I'm Julia, and I'll help you rock yourself the way you were meant to be rocked."

You find it peculiar that this girl who looks and sounds like Julia (despite the weird hair) also has the same name as her, but you don't get to think about it very long before Julia starts to sell you on some of the rockingest speakers you've ever experienced. She turns out to be the best speaker salesperson you've ever had, breaking down each speaker according to how gnarly they'll look in your living room and how many panties will drop with each notch of the volume knob. She even tells you about the tweeters without you having to ask. In the end, you buy a set of kick-ass speakers for a total of $574.77.

"Thank you for helping me improve my life without having to apply for financing," you say to her.

"It's me," Julia whispers. She looks at you gravely. You realize then that it's Julia, your Julia, the one you gave up for dead so long ago.

"But your hair," you say.

"It's dyed," she says. "He made me dye it."

She motions over her shoulder to Irving. You recognize his face from the store's advertisements. He stands at the railing of the upper level watching the store as if he, not the speaker, was king of the Speaker Kingdom.

"Go around back to the loading dock to pick up your speakers, and then call the police," she says.

You do as she says and the police come and take Irving away. Julia is all over the news for the next few weeks, telling her tale of how Irving kept her locked away for months so that he could teach her speaker sales. He filmed that hologram that he showed at the factory because he never had any intention of showing up to collect any ransom or give Julia away. He had no family and no love in his life. All he had was the Speaker Kingdom, and he needed someone to pass it on to after he'd gone.

He kept Julia under constant watch, threatening her life if she should try to escape, while he built up her speaker sales acumen from scratch. She said he kidnapped her because he didn't think he could properly inculcate his knowledge of speaker sales into a subject unless he kept them in captivity. Irving thought that he would give Julia his store after he died, and even wrote it into his will. He never thought he might be taken away from the store while he was still alive.

"You fool!" he screams when the police drag him away. "Now the store will fall to ruin. It could all have been yours had you only been patient. All of it."

But Julia knew she'd have her kingdom. Most convicts once had as much need for a good set of speakers as the next American, and it isn't long before Irving is shivved in prison by a former Speaker Kingdom customer who felt he'd been taken for a ride. When Irving dies, his will is executed and the store is bequeathed to Julia, treasonous queen of the Speaker Kingdom.

Once things calm down, you return to the Speaker Kingdom to see if Julia would like to go on a second date with you. She tells you that with a Speaker Kingdom in need of her rule she has no time for socializing, but as a token of her gratitude to you she gives you a free set of Monster cables.

THE END

Write "Preapocalypse" on Your Time Sheet

Ten years later, you bump into Julia when you end up temping for her at an ad agency. It doesn't feel good to be temping at age forty-three, but you don't want to take full-time work as it will keep you from working on your documentary monologue collection, *Where YOU Were on 9/11*. Even though 9/11 occurred over a decade and a half ago, you still think your piece will be relevant (if you can just manage to get some dickhead who was in the towers to finally talk to you).

"Oh dear," Julia says when you arrive. "You're my temp?"

"I knew your name was kind of familiar for some reason," you say. "So . . . you lived?"

"Is it that obvious?"

You laugh a little too hard. Then you go to your desk.

The day isn't too bad. There aren't too many awkward moments, except for around three p.m. when you come back from a long bathroom break and she says, "I was calling for you but you never came."

At the end of the day, she invites you for a coffee at Starbucks. There she tells you that when the kidnappers tried to cash the check you gave them, the police swooped in and eventually she was saved. You explain to her that you only left her to live or die at the kidnappers' mercy because you were pretty down on the state of current events and you figured, what's the point.

Things are awkward after that. You make a joke that you think is really funny about how many Starbucks there are in the city, the punch line involving a proctologist and a freshly made venti Frappuccino being pulled from an anus, but Julia doesn't laugh. You try to relate to her about both of you being in your forties, but Julia reminds you that she is three years younger than you, and her fortieth birthday isn't for two months.

"We established that on our only date together."

You say, "Oh."

"You're the only one here who is in his forties," Julia says.

You take a sip of your blended beverage.

"Just like you're the only one here who's still temping," Julia adds.

You say, "I thought about you, you know."

"Did you?" she says.

"Yeah," you say. "I used to think that maybe if I had stuck it out and saved you, like really saved you, then things might have turned out a little better for me."

Julia says, "I made you my hero. When I gave them your phone number, you became my hero in that moment. I really built you up in my mind. You blew it."

When she gets up, you say, "Wait. Can I still temp for you tomorrow?"

She's thrown and doesn't answer immediately.

"I need the money," you say.

She looks confused, then says, "Okay. See you tomorrow."

You sit for a while after she leaves, trying to figure out

what you should eat for dinner that night. You browse the prewrapped sandwiches at the counter, but ultimately, you decide to order a pizza when you get home. You're going to have some work this week, so it's okay.

THE END

Your Self-Sabotaging Nature Has Grown So Profound You Suffer from a Split-Personality Disorder So That Sometimes You're Able to Actually Become the Person Who Is Keeping You Down

The next morning, you find in your mail slot a ransom note composed of letters cut out from newspapers and magazines and pasted together to form words. This creeps you out because when you woke up you found all of your newspapers and magazines cut up into pieces and little scraps of paper all over the floor and you weren't sure why. The note tells you to deliver the ransom money to an address. It's your own apartment. The note says that Julia will be there when you deliver the money.

You hunt around your apartment, which is not very big, until you open the coat closet and find Julia bound and gagged.

"What the fuck?" she says when you untie her.

"Holy shit—you've been here the whole time?"

"You put me here, dick."

"And we didn't talk on the phone?"

She grabs from the floor the gag that was in her mouth and chucks it at you. It's wet.

"That whole phone call must have been in my head," you say.

Julia wants some explanations.

"I'm sorry. I've always been kind of prone to sabotaging

myself, and after a while self-sabotage gets really time-consuming because you have to pretend that you actually want to succeed at whatever you're trying to make yourself fail at. So I developed this other personality that appears anytime there's anything that might be good in my life. He must have thought I had a real chance with you, so he abducted you, probably assuming that my real personality would blow the rescue or not bother to save you, and you'd never want to see me again."

Julia asks if your other personality does this a lot.

"Only when things look really promising for me. Like the time I was up for a really great part in a play, and on the day of the final callback my other personality made me go out and get really drunk beforehand."

Julia says that sounds less like split-personality disorder and more like alcoholism.

"Then there was Free Cone Day at Ben & Jerry's. I was all ready to go out and get a free ice cream cone when my other personality picked up a hammer and made me slam myself in the head with it until I was unconscious."

Julia says, "Oh."

"I was out cold for all of Free Cone Day. Then there was the time I was close to getting this really great apartment that would have saved me a lot of money, but I had to get to the rental office before closing. Just as I was about to leave, my other personality grabbed a steak knife and made me stab myself in the thigh over and over again."

Julia says, "Holy fuck."

"It will stop at nothing to prevent me from pursuing a promising opportunity."

Julia blushes. "So I guess you and I are a promising opportunity."

"Looks like it," you say.

"Well, when I encounter your other personality I'll have to thank him for letting me know," Julia says.

She leans in to kiss you, but your other personality makes you get up and jump out your window. You fall eleven flights and shatter your spine. Julia stays by your bedside while you recuperate, and the nursing staff watches with glee as your love takes hold and grows strong, and your other personality can't do a damn thing about it because you're in a body cast.

THE END

Will You Help Your Country?

Using your superhuman ability to kill in the name of love, you rescue Julia from the kidnappers and the two of you live happily together until the government comes calling.

"We watched you take down those kidnappers via satellite. You have quite a gift. Will you help your country?" the man from the government asks.

"Sorry," you say. "That was Love Vigilantism. It was my love for my girlfriend that gave me that power."

"Don't you love her anymore?" the man from the government asks.

"More than ever," you say with a smile. "But no one is trying to keep us apart. I'm not a Love Vigilante anymore. Now I'm just a guy in love. I'm sorry, but I'm really in the weeds tonight."

You tend to your other tables and the man from the government pays his bill, tipping poorly, and leaves. He tucks his card in with the bill, the note on the back of it reads: *In case you change your mind.*

At the end of your shift, you go home and find the place ransacked and Julia gone. You search the mess for a clue as to who might be responsible, and you find an Al-Qaeda membership card with an address in Iraq. You call up the man from the government and tell him you're in.

It's only after you've used your bloody powers of Love Vigilantism to bring peace to Iraq by wiping out the insurgency and ending the seemingly unstoppable civil war that you find Julia and she tells you the man from the government set the whole thing up.

"It wasn't Al-Qaeda. It was Washington that took me," she says. "Washington, D.C.!"

So you go home and kill everyone in Washington. Then your powers go away and you go back to waiting tables again. Eventually, you propose and Julia accepts.

THE END

The Man in the Towers

At first, you tell Reggie you aren't sure. "It's too danger-ous," you say.

But the real reason is that you're afraid to return to freedom and try to get your life back on track after so many years underground. You don't want to have to go back out there and try to make something of yourself. You like being a ghost.

Reggie sits on the bed with you, his head in his hands.

"Jesus, this is making my head hurt," he says. "My head hasn't hurt this much since 9/11."

You ask him where he was on 9/11.

"Tower One," he says.

You think you might faint.

"Can you tell me about it?" you ask.

"Only if you escape with me," Reggie says.

With Reggie's account of his time in Tower One, you'll finally have the centerpiece to your one-man show. You'll finally be able to finish the piece and make your mark in the world of theater.

"After what you just said to me, I'll follow you any-where," you say.

You and Reggie escape that night and hitchhike across state lines, trying to put as much distance between you and the rest of the kidnappers as possible. After a few nights of running, you finally find a town that looks like you can stay in it for a while, and you bunk down in a hotel room where he finally shows you his face. He has some acne.

That night you ask Reggie to tell you about his experi-ence on September 11th.

"I heard a loud rumble," he says.

"Wait!" you say. You don't have a tape recorder, so you grab the notepad off the nightstand and start scribbling. "Okay, go ahead."

"I heard a loud rumble," he says.

"Uh-huh."

"A wall support came loose and hit me in the head," he says.

"Uh-huh."

"Seventeen days later, I woke up in the hospital."

You ask Reggie to repeat that and he does.

"How'd you get out of the building before it fell?" you ask.

"They say my cubicle mate carried me down. All sixty-two stories. He was just a temp. I never even got his name. You want a good story, go find that guy."

You ask Reggie if he knows where that guy is, and he shrugs.

"The doctor told me when I came in I had crapped my pants, too," he says. "Man, that temp was a hero."

You make sure you've got it all.

"So on September 11th, 2001, you heard a rumble. You got hit in the head. You crapped your pants. Then seventeen days later you woke up in the hospital."

"That'll do 'er," Reggie says.

"Have you kept in contact with anyone else who you used to work with?" you ask.

"I kind of lost touch when I got into this kidnapping thing," he says. "It's hard to hang onto old colleagues when you move into a new field. Hey, speaking of new fields, we gotta get jobs!"

Reggie folds open the local paper and takes out two pens. He circles in blue the jobs he's going to apply for to-morrow. He uses the red pen to circle the jobs *you* should apply for tomorrow. Within half an hour you see there is a whole lot of red on that paper. He asks your opinion on certain listings occasionally, but you're distracted. You can't help but wonder what's going on back at the safe house.

THE END

Saved by an Urchin

When you step outside Luigi's abortion clinic, a small, raggedy-looking boy is waiting to sell you a box of candy.

"Did you just get a baby abortioned?" he asks you.

"My friend did," you say.

"Didn't you think you could love your baby?" the kid says.

"Not right now," you say.

"At least you knew. Sometimes I miss my daddy so much I wish my mom had gotten *me* abortioned," he says. "Wanna buy a box of candy? I'm supposed to say it's for my basketball team's uniforms, but it isn't really."

You give him a dollar for a box of Milk Duds, and you open it and offer him some but he refuses. You ask him if his daddy is dead or just gone.

"Gone," he says. "I keep wondering what I could have done to make him stay. How I could have made him proud. Sometimes I feel like what's the point of doing anything if I don't have a daddy who's gonna be proud of me for it."

You tell him it's hard to make some dads proud, even when they stick around. Then you get an idea.

"I tell you what," you say. "If you sell fifty thousand boxes of that candy and you give me the money, I'll be so proud I'll join Big Brothers and take you out *every* weekend."

"You just watch!" the kid says. He then takes off running down the street, stopping to ask everyone he sees if they'd like to buy some candy. He comes back in a half hour with $50,000 in cash.

"You just saved a girl's life!" you say. "What's your name?"

"Billy!" he says, brimming with pride.

You take Billy with you to the kidnappers. When you show them the money, the kidnappers are impressed. "That sure was fast," they say.

"It wasn't me. It was my little brother here," you say, rubbing Billy's hair.

The kidnappers fawn all over Billy, telling him what a great little salesman he is and how proud his big brother must be. Then after Julia is untied she comes over and kisses him on the cheek.

"Thanks for rescuing me," she says. "Boy, am I hungry."

The kidnappers tousle Billy's hair and say good-bye to the three of you before escaping with the money in their helicopter. You and Julia take Billy to Chuck E. Cheese's for dinner, and you all have such a good time that you and Julia make a plan to take him there every weekend. After a year, Billy's mother asks if you'd like to buy him for $10,000. You and Julia agree to pitch in for it, but you only come up with $3,000 between you, so you have Billy sell some more candy and raise the remaining $7,000. You pay Billy's mother off, arrange for the adoption, and you and Julia get married at Chuck E. Cheese's. The animatronic mouse that plays the ukelele officiates (that's legal in your state).

THE END

Tell Your Dad It's Time for You to Stand on Your Own Two Feet

"It's time for me to stand on my own two feet, Dad," you say. "Maybe I will screw this up. But if I keep letting you bail me out because I'm afraid to fail, I'm never gonna learn how to try. That girl might die, but at least I'll have done my best."

Your dad gets out of his car and joins you on the sidewalk. Neither of you is looking at each other. It feels like you're saying good-bye.

"What's gonna happen to me, then?" he asks, staring off into the expanse of the street. "Your mother thinks I'm the mistake of her life. Now if you don't need me to rescue you anymore, what good am I?"

"You're my dad," you say. You put your hand on his shoulder. "I need you to be proud of me."

He looks down at your hand and smiles. "Proud of you," he says. "I could get used to that."

You check your watch. "I'd better get going now, Dad. I've got a girl to save. Can I borrow your car?"

Your Dad looks you in the eye and says, "Drive carefully."

If you want to drive carefully, go to page 150.

If you want to drive recklessly, go to page 87.

The Good-bye Hostage

You go to sleep that night with Reggie's arms around you, his body spooning yours, the cotton of his hood soft against the back of your head. It is the best sleep you've had in months (with Julia gone, you are able to use the bed again). In the morning, Reggie's gone.

Marcus and Sam take off soon after, on the same night, complaining that it's too depressing being around you.

"His dad won't even pay fifty grand to get him back," Marcus explains to Chet. "What's wrong with this guy that his parents won't take out another mortgage just to get him back?"

"His girl left him," Sam adds. "Reggie left him. And he just sits down there without a care in the world. Face it, Chet, this guy loves being a hostage."

For a while it's just you and Chet. You sit in your basement, listening to him pace around on the floor above. After so many years living underneath the pitter-patter of those four kidnappers, the sound of just that one pair of footsteps is enough to break your heart.

One day, Chet comes down to the basement in between meals. He offers you a sip off the bottle of whiskey from which he's clearly been drinking very aggressively. The two of you sit side by side on the floor and you take generous swigs from the bottle, though you don't stand a chance of catching up to Chet.

"What's a kidnapper if he kidnaps someone no one comes lookin' for?" he asks. "We're nothin' but two guys sittin' around a house."

Chet seems determined that kidnapping is not right for him and it's time he made some changes in his life. You try to reassure Chet that things will turn around for him soon. For four years you've had all your decisions made for you, and you're terrified that without a kidnapper you'll be sent back out into freedom, where you'll have to try and make something of yourself. You give him a long pep talk, but when the bottle is finished, Chet gets up to leave.

"I'm sorry I took all these years away from you," Chet says. "It was all for nothing."

Then he shuts the door and heads upstairs. You fall asleep listening to his defeated footsteps through the ceiling.

The next day, you stop hearing footsteps. Chet doesn't bring you breakfast or lunch, either. At dinnertime, when you try the door to the basement, it's unlocked.

No way would he just give up on the kidnapping without telling you first. You're a team! He was just drunk and forgot to lock the door. It's probably a test, you decide. Chet's just waiting outside to pick you off if you try to run. You're hungry, though, so you race upstairs and hoard food to bring back to the basement before Chet returns.

The next couple of weeks pass with no sign of Chet (though he's probably coming by to check on you while you're asleep. It's quite possible). You run upstairs for food every day, certain that at any moment he could come home and kill you for getting out.

Eventually the food runs out and you start to waste away in the basement. You're on the brink of death when a bank appraiser comes to the house and finds you. She phones the police and you're returned to society. The media makes a spectacle of you and you get many letters from people who tell you you're very brave. You go back to your life and take an office job, doing what little you can to make up for lost time. During the long days withering away at your cubicle you hold a glimmer of hope that the police will capture Chet and you'll get the chance to ask him to his face just what sort of monster he is to have left you to fend for yourself like this.

THE END

You're the One That You Want

You press Play on the DVD and you watch yourself masturbate. You've never seen a videotape of yourself masturbating, or having sex of any kind really, and you're startled by how turned on you are. You begin to masturbate to the tape of yourself masturbating, trying to time your orgasm to the moment of your orgasm on the tape. You manage to hit the moment almost exactly, coming just a second after you come on the DVD. The strength of the orgasm is unprecedented. You just lie there for a while afterward, marveling at what you've discovered today. At age thirty-three a whole new door has been opened into your sexuality, and you can't wait to run right through it. The only thing you want now is to find the person who sent you that DVD so that you can get him to give you a recording of the past few minutes. You want to masturbate to a DVD of you masturbating to a DVD of you masturbating. You want this more than you want to take your next breath. The snake has been waiting a mighty long time to eat its own tail, and the snake is hungry.

If you want to find the man who made the DVD and offer him the $50,000 to continue to give you DVDs of you masturbating to yourself, go to page 82.

If you want to find the man who made the DVD and kill him, go to page 153.

Unleash the Dickwad Within

When you step out of Luigi's abortion clinic, you spot a flyer for a personal development workshop that reads:

DO YOU WANT LOTS OF MONEY AND A BEAUTIFUL SPOUSE WHO LOVES YOU BECAUSE YOU ARE YOUR OWN BOSS? THERE IS A GEYSER OF PERSONAL PO-TENTIAL *WAITING TO BURST OUT OF YOU. FIND OUT HOW TO* COAT THE WORLD *WITH* AN EXPLO-SION OF YOU. *ATTEND* MONUMENT LIVING ED-UCATION WORKSHOPS *TODAY!*

According to the flyer, there's one just around the corner that's starting right now. If you hurry, you can make it.

You burst into the workshop and take a seat. The proctor has just begun a ninety-minute introduction begging you to congratulate yourselves for finally doing what's necessary to show the world what you're capable of. Then he has everyone get up in front of the room one at a time and say what they want to achieve.

One guy wants to get up the nerve to ask his secretary out on a date. The next guy is a manager of a CVS and he wants to buy his own ranch one day. The lady after him wants to move out of her ex-husband's basement. Then you get up there.

"I want to raise fifty thousand dollars in ransom money by midnight tonight so I can save a girl who's been kidnapped. I only have five hours left. How do I do it?"

The proctor tells you that you've come to the right

place, because Monument Living Education Workshops will give you the focus, the discipline, and the network of connections to raise more ransom money than a kidnapper could ever even dream about. "The secret is in your body language," he says.

The next hour is spent critiquing your classmates' posture, with the proctor using a laser pointer to show which parts of each of your bodies are telling the world to kick sand in your face, and which body parts get you the good table at ritzy restaurants. Then he shows you a slide show of people with nice hair and strong jawlines looking wealthy, and he points out that that's the kind of posture that makes people do stuff.

"But how will better posture get me fifty thousand dollars before midnight, which is only around three hours away now, by the way?" you ask.

"You can't expect to raise fifty thousand dollars in three hours just because you've got good posture!" the proctor says with a laugh. "You need eye contact, too!"

The next hour is devoted to a demonstration of how to look someone in the eye. He has class members come up and role play, where they pretend to ask each other out on dates and demand that landlords return security deposits. By a show of hands, it is unanimously agreed that those who use eye contact are far more persuasive than those who do not.

"But I only have an hour left," you say. "How do I get the fifty thousand dollars that's going to save that poor girl?"

The proctor tells you that a lot of times, if we can't figure out how to get something done in our lives, it's probably because there are negative people surrounding us who are holding us back. We can't surmount our obstacles if we

don't know where they are, he says. You're told to make a
list of all the people in your life who are keeping you from
doing whatever you want, whenever you want. You're surprised when, just underneath your mom and dad, you write
Julia's name.

That's when the epiphany hits you. The obligation to
rescue Julia from her kidnappers is plugging up the geysers
of personal potential that could coat the entire world in a
deep puddle of just how awesome you really are! It is your
duty to look Julia in the eye and tell her that she either has
to join Monument and unlearn her negative, vampiric, personal potential geyser-stoppering ways, or she's got to get
out of your life. Unfortunately, by the time you have this
epiphany it's after midnight and Julia is likely already dead.

"It's too late for her," the proctor says. "But not for you."

You hastily write the proctor a check for eleven hundred dollars and in return he gives you a DVD and a guide-
book that will teach you how to convince your loved ones
that they are diseased and that they must join Monument
or risk being cut out of your life forever.

THE END

A More Sensitive Safe House

Chet is ashamed. So are Marcus and Sam. They are admitting as much to Reggie.

"As far as I'm concerned," Chet tells Reggie, "I'm the one who let that girl go."

"No, it was me," says Marcus. "I might as well have just opened the front door and kissed her good-bye as she left."

"Please," Sam says. "I practically drove her to the Amtrak station and gave her money for the bar car. I loathe myself so much right now."

"Wow," Reggie says. "I really thought you guys would be madder than this."

After Julia was discovered to have escaped, the other kidnappers demanded that Reggie tell them exactly how she got past him. He was forced to admit that he is gay, and that he had been distracted at the time of Julia's escape because he was in the process of making secret, forbidden love to you in a position that was complicated and required most of his concentration. Julia managed to get hold of his assault rifle and crack him on the back of the head, knocking him unconscious and pinning you underneath his dead weight. His fellow kidnappers were far more understanding than he feared.

"What kind of a safe house is this," Chet says, shaking his head in dismay, "if we don't feel safe enough to admit who we truly are to one another? We have clearly created an environment here where you felt you had to hide your heart from us, Reggie. Had we known that you were carrying on an affair with one of our captives, we would have known to take you off guard duty since no one can expect you to remain vigilant when you're caught up in the dizzying early stages of a love affair."

"Not to mention, all of his effort was probably going into keeping the affair a secret from us," Marcus adds.

"If you think about it, Reggie was the one we've been keeping locked away."

They all sit and think about it for a second. Then they ask Reggie for his forgiveness.

"From now on we'll remember that when we tell what we think is just a harmless joke at the breakfast table, we might actually be forcing someone we care about to live a lie," Chet says.

They all hug and cry some.

When Reggie comes downstairs to see you, he is walking on air. "Those kidnappers are the most caring, understanding, and bighearted kidnappers in the whole wide world. I'm the luckiest kidnapper on earth," he exclaims. "Let's escape!"

"Escape?" you ask.

Reggie explains that no matter how much he loves his fellow kidnappers, now that he's out to them he needs to be out to the whole world. "I want to go back into society and live my life as I truly am, for the first time ever. Come with me. Let's find out how we are as a couple without any padlocks or assault rifles."

If you want to escape with Reggie, go to page 121.

If you want to stay in the basement, go to page 128.

Thanks for Being You

After the old Italian man disappears, you close your eyes and shout up at the heavens, "Why is it so hard to abort a baby?!"

When you open your eyes, Kim is gone and you find yourself back in the town where you grew up. Except it is no longer the idyllic Anytown, USA, that it used to be. Now it is impoverished and crowded with vacant buildings and rundown shacks and there's graffiti everywhere.

"All over the place," you whisper to yourself as you take in all the graffiti. "Even on the tree that once held my beloved tire swing."

A voice bellows from behind you that you never swung from any tree in this town, because you were never born. You turn around and you see that the voice is coming from a big fat ghost in a bloody robe.

"Is this supposed to show me what life would be like without me?" you ask.

The ghost shrugs. "Pretty much. They just send me down here when someone's trying to abort a baby. It's a new program. I'm here to show you what the world would be like if your mom had aborted you."

"But I just don't want to have to be a dad yet," you say. "Especially since I have to save this girl and all."

The ghost says, "Look! Your mother is digging a latrine!"

Across the street you see your mother looking filthy, digging into the ground with a shovel.

"Since she never had you, she never felt any need to make anything special of her life. Now she digs latrines."

You watch your mother take a break and light a cigarette.

"And look, here comes your dad!"

You father pulls up in a pickup truck and gets out to hand your mother her lunch box. Then he gives her a kiss. The truck reads KEVIN & CECILLE'S A PLUSS LATRINE DIGGING. Kevin and Cecille are your parents.

"Neither of them really saw any reason to go for the gold, not without a son to pass on their dreams to, so they opened this latrine-digging business and are just making ends meet."

You say to the ghost, "They look so happy and in love. Does this mean they would have continued to love each other if they had aborted me?"

You watch them talk and then just before your father hops back into the truck, he says something that makes your mother burst out laughing. Then he drives off.

The ghost realizes that he has created an uncomfortable situation. "So anyway," he says, "if you want your mother to stop digging latrines and, um, if you wanna see all this graffiti go away, I suggest you go back and convince your girlfriend to have that baby."

"But if I go back, my mother and father will be miserable," you say. "Look how happy my mother is without me having been born. I'm not so sure it's a good idea that I exist. Maybe I should just stay in this ghost world, huh?"

The ghost looks at her. There is a glow about her.

"Yeah, but the graffiti," the ghost says.

You keep your eyes on your mother, taking in as much of her as you can. It's such a marvel to see her truly happy.

"Man, they sure must hate me. They really used to love each other. Before I came along."

The ghost tries to come up with some way to steer you toward going back and having your baby. But he can't think of anything to say except, "This is a tough break, kid. Sorry."

Turn to the ghost and he'll hold you tight.

THE END

Never Say Live!

While Kim waits on the sidewalk, you hoist yourself up on the fire escape and ascend to the abortionist's window. You peek into his living room, which is crowded with decorative ceramics and gleaming with plastic slipcovers, to see the abortionist leaning over the back of a chair where his wife plays with a baby. You knock on the glass.

The wife yelps and places her hand over her chest, looking like she might faint where she's sitting. The abortionist goes to the window.

"You almost give'a my wife heart attack. She almost drop'a my grandson," he says. "Get down or I call'a the police."

"Please," you say to him. "This is a very special circumstance. If you don't abort my ex-girlfriend's baby tonight, the girl I just started dating might die."

The abortionist invites you in and his wife puts her grandson in a crib. He tells you his name is Luigi, and he has his wife fix you a large plate of spaghetti and meatballs, which you eat at his kitchen table while explaining your predicament.

You tell Luigi about the kidnapping, and about how Kim wanted you to be sure to save Julia so that in case she decides to keep the baby, it won't have to be ashamed of its father. Then when you pushed her to abort right away, she said she wanted the baby gone no matter what because she couldn't stand to have the baby of such a coward.

Luigi throws up his hands. "So what! You go save'a that girl tonight and come back tomorrow, I kill baby. *Capiche?*"

"No," you say. "See, Kim wants to abort right now because she thinks I'm a terrible person. But if I end up saving Julia tonight, Kim might change her mind about aborting because I'll be this big hero and she'll be excited to have the baby of a hero. Knowing that, I might just let Julia die to avoid having to be a dad. So if you don't abort that baby right now, you might be murdering a grown woman. Can you live with that?"

Luigi looks disturbed. "You sure'a you the father?" he asks.

You say yes.

The abortionist looks at his wife. She nods once.

"Come'a downstairs," he says.

He leads you down to his clinic and opens the door for Kim.

"I give'a you abortion now," he says to Kim. "With'a him as the father, I understand why you no wanna waste any time. I get'a that'a baby outta you!"

And so the abortionist kicks you out and you're free to save Julia without the added pressure of a child's personality development being dependent on your success.

But there's still the matter of that ransom money.

If you want join a self-actualization group and learn how to attain vast wealth and riches, go to page 132.

If you want to get help from a fatherless little boy, go to page 124.

Women Who Love Men Who Aren't Rich

The kidnappers call at midnight and order you to bring the money to the old abandoned ketchup factory on the outskirts of town. When you arrive in the vast, empty space, you find four men with guns surrounding Julia, who is tied to a chair. You give them the money and Julia is released. She runs into your embrace and promises her devotion to you.

While you hold her in your arms, their leader, who introduces himself only as "Chet," asks you how you got the money so fast.

"My rich friend gave it to me," you say.

"So you're just the delivery boy," Chet says with a laugh. He says to Julia, "You're hugging the wrong guy. It's like someone just bought you a fancy dinner and you're going to bed with the waiter. You make bad decisions."

The kidnappers walk out, cackling over what they perceive to be Julia's poor decision to give herself to you, completely discounting the fact that you put yourself in harm's way while all Danny did was supply the money— but whatever. As their laughter continues out in the parking lot, you feel Julia's embrace of you slacken a bit, but she's probably just tired.

Now that she's free, Julia hastily proves her devotion to you by having sex with you and becoming pregnant with your child. It should be a joyful time, but as her pregnancy progresses you keep hearing those kidnappers laughing at Julia. You imagine them gathered behind you, trying to stifle their giggling while you learn to breathe at Lamaze class, or while you look at the baby's little arm during the amniocentesis. Their laughter follows you everywhere, because deep down you think people are right to laugh at Julia. She really did choose the wrong guy.

You can't help but feel as if Danny is somehow the real father of your child. The child was spawned from your seed, certainly, but Julia's womb was available to you only because her life was spared through the benevolence of Danny. And now that you are in his employ, your child will be fed with Danny's money. After all these years of viewing Danny from afar as the embodiment of the life you could have had, he is now in control of your life and everything it has to offer you. He hovers over you like a god, bestowing whatever happiness you may enjoy. This is all too much to bear and it brings you to the decision that Danny must be eliminated. You have a year in his employ to exact your vengeance. It will be just enough time.

Within just a few months of employment, you become a legend in the halls of Wipe-face.com. The staff members ("facewipes," they're called) have heard the rumor that you helped Danny come up with the Wipe-face concept, and want to know why you're here. Why, if you are capable of the level of brilliance that could create a multimillion-dollar online property devoted to pictures of people on toilets, have you not built your own Silicon Valley empire? Why are you working as an admin assistant at the company you helped found?

The mystery draws them to you. You represent the unexplainable ingredient that took a simple scatological concept and made them all millionaires. You manipulate their reverence and turn them against Danny, making them believe that you are the true creator of Wipe-face.com, and Danny is nothing more than the grinning fraud at the helm.

On the eve of your one-year anniversary at the company, just hours before you are to be released from your agreement with Danny, you gather the facewipes and lead them to Danny's office. He is sitting behind his desk when you arrive, looking as if he'd summoned you.

"I'm sorry, old friend," you say. "I can't have you controlling my fate any longer."

"But who's to say this isn't my doing as well?" he says. "Perhaps I brought you on only because I knew you'd one day turn on me."

You look into Danny's eyes and you see no fear, only sadness. He wanted this. He planned even this. Clearly, as you'd always hoped, his vast wealth and unlimited power have only made him more miserable with every day (it happens!), and he craves only death. The only way to defy him is to let him live, but your fury takes control and you unleash his employees upon him.

The facewipes club Danny and eat him, as is custom when power is transferred at a dot-com. With Danny gone, the company is yours. You quickly run it into the ground because you don't know how to run companies.

THE END

Turn to Drugs

You tell them to kill Julia, and you beg them to let you and your dad leave before they do it. The kidnappers concede, and you don't hear a gunshot until you've made it all the way to the car. That's when you discover the other bag of money still in the front seat. You tell your Dad that you're keeping the money, and he doesn't argue since he knows he ruined everything. You and he stop speaking after this.

You use the money to develop a severe cocaine addiction, the kind of addiction where you start making friends with people who are different nationalities than you, like from weird places in Eastern Europe even. You always have three girlfriends at once and you try to keep a bobcat as a house pet, but it goes wild so you lock it in your bedroom and wait for it to get quiet in there. After four months of nonstop partying, your money is all gone but the addiction is still there and so is the bobcat, so you go into Narcotics Anonymous, where you discover that Julia is still alive.

"I once staged my own kidnapping," she's telling the group on your first night at NA. "It was all to get this guy I went on a date with to get me and my cokehead friends, a bunch of strangers who were of different nationalities than me, some money so we could buy some more cocaine."

She doesn't see you there.

"He was a really nice guy, too. Really cute. I made him think they killed me. When I watched him leave, knowing what I'd done to him, knowing how nice he was and how sweet on our first date, I wished they *had* killed me. I wished I could have just gone on a second date with him, like normal people do. But I already had a boyfriend who was really jealous. My boyfriend's name was cocaine."

The others in the group tell Julia to keep coming back. Then they look to you and ask if you want to share anything. Julia gasps when she sees you. You stand up.

"I was going to say that I started doing cocaine after I tried to rescue a girl from kidnappers and she ended up getting killed, but she's over there," you say. Then you sit back down. They tell you to keep coming back.

You and Julia go through the program together, and you forgive her because you know what sort of grip cocaine can have on a person. Eventually, you go on a second date, but all you talk about is how great it used to be to do cocaine. You go your separate ways, her back to Chicago and you back to your dad, with whom you've reconciled now that you know he wasn't responsible for a girl's death.

THE END

Use Your Power of Love for Evil

After you use your power of love to murder the kidnappers and rescue Julia, a man approaches you and asks if you'll help him bring young girls over the border from Mexico.

"Once they're here, we enslave them and force them into prostitution," the man says.

"That sounds really evil," you say.

"But there's a lot of money in it," the man says. "We just need you to use your otherworldly powers to unleash a fury of pain and torment upon the border patrolmen any time they try to look in the back of the truck."

"Sorry," you say. "My power is a kind of love vigilantism and it only works when something is trying to come between me and the girl I love."

The human trafficker thinks about this. "But how will you hang onto your love if you can't provide her with the life she deserves? You could say that being poor is an enemy to your love, and insuring that a branch of the sex slave trade makes it across the border without any problems in exchange for lots of money is the same as striking down a dastardly villain trying to tear you apart."

"That makes perfect sense!" you concede. You drop your tray on the ground, toss your server's apron, and tell your manager he can wait the rest of your tables himself.

So you agree to protect the human traffickers, and it isn't long before your human trafficking ring yields you and Julia a great deal of money. You're providing her with a life you and she had only ever dreamed about, and her love for

you only grows stronger and stronger. Until she finds another woman's hair on your sweater.

"You're cheating on me, aren't you?" she says.

You don't want her to think you're unfaithful, so you tell
her the truth about the human trafficking and the girls who
are being forced into prostitution, yielding you and Julia
vast riches.

"My God," she says. "How could you do such a thing?"

"I'm just trying to keep poverty from tearing you away
from me!" you say. Then you leave in a huff.

That day at the border, a patrolman tries to look in the
back of the truck. You try to use your murderous talent to
rip his stomach out of his body, but nothing happens. The
patrolman shoots you once in the chest. As you lie dying,
you realize that Julia stopped loving you, and so you were
left powerless. You are thankful that you are far from medical attention, and you only wish that you could use your
powers one last time to speed your own death along. You
want nothing more than to leave this loveless world as fast
as you can.

THE END

A Whole Bunch of Cautionary Tales in Tight Pants and Bustiers

After driving very carefully on your way to the ransom drop, you find you have some time to kill so you pull over to take in the view at a scenic point along the highway and exult.

"I'm making my daddy proud of me!" you shout into the canyon below. The returning echo is shattered by a nearby voice.

"Must be nice," a woman says.

You climb to a higher viewing plateau and you find a loose gathering of men and women sitting and lying on benches. Some of them are coupled up and groping each other, while others are sitting alone, looking anxious. All of them are dressed in exciting going-out-on-a-Friday-night clothes, even though it's the middle of a sunny weekday and they're all at the scenic overlook off the shoulder of a highway.

The woman who spoke to you looks very inviting in her lycra top and heels. "My mom and dad never showed any pride in me," she says. "Never really made me feel like I had a right to their attention."

The far end of her bench is occupied by another woman and a man, both of them naked from the waist up. The woman straddles the man's lap and she looks bored by the man's mouth on her breasts.

"I'm betting no one around here ever knew what it meant to make his or her daddy proud," the woman in the lycra top continues. "Guess that's why we all come out here to a highway rest stop, looking for just a little bit of a stranger's attention before we all continue on our separate ways. That's about all we think we're entitled to."

"You all come here every day?" you ask, averting your eyes from the couple at the end of the bench, who are now having intercourse through their open zippers.

"Jesus, we're not pervs. We have to work sometimes." She laughs. "This is just a place to come when it gets too long since we've let ourselves be touched and it gets so cold that we start to shiver in the sunshine."

You look around at the couples in their various states of undress. The sun looks warm on their skin.

"So how about it?" the woman in the lycra top asks. "You want some company?"

If you want to have sex with the woman at the highway rest stop, go to page 192.

If you want to keep driving carefully to the ransom drop, go to page 91.

Love the One You're With

"I'm sorry," you tell Reggie. "Julia and I have been together for so long. I couldn't imagine my life in this basement without her."

Reggie responds with a smirk.

"And what about your life outside of this basement?" he asks.

"I have to live the life I have right now," you say. "I can't make a choice based on wild possibilities."

He laughs now. "Not so wild as you think."

"What are you saying, Reggie?"

Reggie says that Chet is considering giving up and finally letting you both go. They're all going to vote on it tonight. But everyone's pretty sick of waiting it out and it seems pretty certain that the two of you will get out.

"You could be free by the end of the week," Reggie says. "Still ready to tie the knot?"

If you want to go through with the wedding, go to page 86.

If you want to tell Reggie he can do what he wants to you if he convinces the kidnappers to vote against a release, go to page 95.

Kill the Witness

You get a call at midnight telling you where to bring the money. You ask the kidnapper if he can bring a DVD of earlier in the evening, when you masturbated to the DVD of you masturbating, and he says he'll see what he can do.

You meet the kidnapper behind the Safeway at midnight, as he instructed. He pulls up in a long black Mercedes and he is very well dressed.

"Well look at what you have gone and done," he says when he peeks into your bag of money.

"I suppose you're wondering what this was all about," he goes on. "I am a very wealthy and very eccentric man. I like to play with people. I've been watching you secretly for quite some time. In you I saw a man who was absolutely crippled by his own fear of the future. Every day you shrunk from any decision that might be put to you so as to always hang onto the possibility that something better might come along. I decided to force you to make some very important choices. The game was that for once, someone else's life would be at stake, and it would be up to you to make big decisions about your own life, or else an innocent girl would die. And here you are." He holds up the bag, victorious. "You've won the game!"

After he sets Julia free from the back of his limousine, you stab him in the stomach with the steak knife you brought with you.

"Why did you do that?" Julia asks while you root through his pockets for the DVD he promised to bring. "He already let me go."

You tell Julia about masturbating to the DVD of yourself, and about the strength of your orgasm. "I considered
just asking him to keep sending DVDs of me masturbating.
But something didn't feel right. And I realized the only
thing that could make my orgasms stronger would be if
there were absolutely no one else alive who had been witness to those images. I needed to close the circle. So, you
see, he had to die."

You and Julia don't talk on the ride home. You drop her
off, and then you race home to masturbate to the DVD
again to see if your theory was correct. Gloriously enough,
it was.

THE END

You Used to Be Somebody!

It gets hard sometimes. Just like any marriage, there are times when you feel so far apart from each other you can't remember what ever brought you together in the first place. Sometimes, when your students are driving you crazy and Julia is at work all night with yet another deadline, not only does it feel like you never spent five years locked away in a life-or-death situation together, it feels like you never even met. It was during such a time when you decided to go looking for Chet.

The police never found him. Marcus and Sam were killed in the raid, and Reggie was arrested a day later. But Chet got away. You need to see him. You need to remember that there once was a time when you lived every day like it was your last. So you hire a private detective who tracks Chet down and arranges a meeting between the two of you at a greasy spoon diner near the airport.

Chet arrives at the table fifteen minutes late and wearing a busboy's uniform. He explains that after the private investigator tracked him down and extended your invitation to have lunch, he had to get a job at the diner you suggested in order to be a step ahead of any potential plot to capture him. He's been working there for a month, he says, and everyone's really nice. He wants to know what this is about.

You're startled to finally see his face. "I always imagined what you might look like. You're blonder than I thought," you say. "How are you?"

He's fine. Is that it?

"Are you still doing abductions?" you ask.

No, he says. Yours was the last.

"That makes me feel good," you say. "Like it meant something. It meant something to me. Was it special to you? Or was it just a kidnapping gone bad?"

He starts to explain that he's done a lot of kidnappings and—

"But for me," you interrupt. "It was the last time I was part of something really big. The past decade has been a long process of me just settling down and accepting what life has in store for me. After we escaped from you, I gave up on a lot of things. Julia did, too. I'm teaching drama in a high school now and it's like I never even wanted to be an actor. Julia took work at an ad agency and they love her there and I can't remember the last time she sent out her clips looking for journalism work."

He asks if kids are on the horizon.

"To be honest, we don't talk about it. Not like we're avoiding it. It just doesn't occur to us. Sometimes I think the only reason we're together is because of the kidnapping. That was my big life event and I want to keep her close so I don't have to forget. I don't know if she feels the same way. We don't talk about it."

He says that she does feel the same way. Or at least, she did eight months ago when she tracked him down and asked him to lunch the same way you did. He notes your surprise and says that it shouldn't be a shock. A kidnapping is a very exciting, life-changing event and it's only natural that you would both want to reunite with others who shared the experience with you. It's probably why people who see UFOs always want to track one another down and talk about it.

"I guess we need you to verify that we were once a part

of something big," you say. "That we were once involved in a matter of life and death. You really would have killed us, wouldn't you have?"

Chet affirms that he would have killed you, then he tells you that his break is over and that you should go home and talk to your wife. Your whole life is a matter of life and death, he says, and just because no one's outside your door with an assault rifle doesn't mean you can't live as if there was.

You thank him. He nods and clears the plate off the table. You pay your bill, go out to your car, and you drive happily to your very safe house.

THE END

He Likes to Watch

You continue hunting around your apartment, removing the grates from air vents and checking behind picture frames, until you take apart the smoke alarm and find a tiny surveillance camera, no bigger than a cigarette, aimed at your bed. You look closely. Engraved in the camera's casing are the words *Deke's Surveillance*. You find a listing online and you go and pay Deke a visit.

You arrive at his shop just as he's closing up. When he sees you through the glass he races to lock the door, but you burst in and slam him against the wall of his shop.

"Don't hit me in the face!" he shouts. "I got a lady and she needs me to stay pretty!"

"You're not that pretty," you tell Deke.

"My lady thinks I'm pretty," he says. "Just let my face stay the way she likes it. If you knew how much I loved this lady, you'd have some mercy."

He really has only average looks, with a slight overbite even, but you tell Deke that if he wants to keep the face his lady is counting on him to maintain, he'd better tell you why he's been watching you.

"I'm not. I'm just recording you," he says.

"For who?"

Deke says, "Him. He never told me his name. He just had me set up the cameras."

"When?" you shout. "When did you set up the cameras?"

"In your current apartment?"

You're stunned. "Were there cameras in my previous apartments?"

Deke realizes he said the wrong thing and he's sputtering

now, begging you to leave his face untouched, telling you how after so many years of being lonely he finally found the lady who can see beauty where everyone else just saw another pair of eyes and a mouth, and please don't blow this for him.

"How long has he been watching me?" you shout. "How long ago did you start spying on me, Deke?"

You grab a stapler and threaten to slam it into Deke's face. It might as well be a beaker of sulfuric acid.

"Fifteen years ago!" Deke screams. "He hired me fifteen years ago. Just please, God, lemme keep my face. It's all my lady wants me for."

Fifteen years? You let go of Deke's shirt lapels, feeling a little woozy. You look away from Deke's very average, really kind of forgettable face, and you look around his darkened office for the first time. Lining the walls are DVDs and videotapes, all with dates on the spines. Many are labeled with one of your old apartment addresses.

"You send these to him?" you say.

"No," he says. "These are backups. He has a direct feed."

The room starts to spin. Your entire life is contained in all that plastic. Every private moment, or what you thought was private.

"This kidnapping . . . ," Deke says. "You have to be careful. He's obsessed with you. After all these years of watching you, now he's drawing you to him. After all these years, God knows what he wants from you."

You suddenly want to get out of Deke's shop. But you still have so many questions that need to be answered. What if the answer is right here in this store?

"Why should I believe you?" you ask. "Why shouldn't I think you're the kidnapper?" You make a fist and aim it at his face.

Deke holds up his hands, cowering. "Because I'm scared of him, too!" Deke says.

If you think Deke knows more and you want to try to beat it out of him, go to page 24.

If you want to race home and wait for this mystery man to call you, go to page 168.

Hell in a Handbasket

"How do I know she's safe?" you say to Chet.

Chet shows you a Polaroid of Julia holding that day's newspaper. You note the fear in her eyes, then you look closely at the newspaper. The headlines all scream about environmental catastrophe and growing hostility from the Middle East, and there's a big picture of the winner of a hot new reality show where people have to stay in a room that smells like piss for a really long time.

"Jesus, this world's going to shit," you say. "What's the point of saving a girl from kidnappers when I'm just gonna make her endure a coming apocalypse."

"Now's not the time to be a doomsayer," Chet says. "If you don't get us the cash, we will murder her today and we will make sure it hurts."

"Will it hurt more than if she's enslaved by lawless tribes who maraud the scorched earth for gasoline so they can make the journey to a mythic water source that hasn't been poisoned? Should I let her live so that she can watch the oceans turn to fire like in that Al Gore movie?"

"Liberal horseshit," Chet says. "You're just trying to duck your responsibility by embracing anti–big business rhetoric. A life is in the balance."

You endorse the back of the check. "Here's your ransom money. If you can cash the check, fine. If not, it's on you. I won't be held responsible for making that girl live another day on this miserable, plague-ridden planet." Then you turn your back on Chet and walk away.

If you want to bump into Julia ten years from now, before the Apocalypse, go to page 113.

If you want to bump into Julia fifteen years from now, after the Apocalypse, go to page 165.

You Did Nothing...in the Name of Love

Kim is wearing a raincoat over her tank top and sweat-pants, the clothes she put on when you shouted up at her window and dragged her out of bed. She stands on the sidewalk in front of her new apartment, her arms folded in front of her, while you explain how you felt when she told you she wanted to stop talking to you. It became clear to you at that moment that it was really over between the two of you, so you decided to just let the police try and rescue Julia because you didn't want to waste another second before racing over here to beg her to take you back.

"But that girl's gonna die," she says.

"Only because I realized how much I need you," you say.

"Holy shit!" she exclaims. "So you're trying to tell me that I killed that girl by telling you I didn't want to talk to you anymore?"

"I didn't mean it like that," you say. "But if we do get back together, at least her death won't have been for nothing."

Kim grabs a trash can and throws it at you, making you stumble off the curb and fall on your back in the street. She then pulls the trash bag from the can and rips it open over you so that you're covered in spoiled lettuce, coffee grounds, and baby diapers. She starts kicking you in the ribs and cursing you. A group of young street toughs wander past and ask to join in. Kim says sure, and she and the fatherless preteens unleash a hurricane of battery upon your ribs and thighs. Then she tells the kids to stop for a second.

"You only think you want me back because you're finally having to deal with the fact that it's over," she screams. "Up until now, you didn't have to worry about me finding someone else or moving on without you because I let you stay so close to me. You wanted out. You made a decision. Here come the consequences!"

She gives the signal and the kids resume stomping on you. Kim walks up her steps, opens her door, then turns to face you. The light from her hallway makes her look angelic.

"I can't believe you used your regret over breaking up with me as an excuse to let that girl die," Kim says. Then she slams the door behind her and one of the street toughs climbs onto your chest and starts jumping his eighty pounds of mass up and down on your lungs.

THE END

Of All the Postapocalyptic Wastelands in All the World...

When you're thrown from the pickup with the rest of the slaves, two mohawked men with shoulder pads chain your ankles and throw you into a wooden cage. They tell you that your master is on her way and you'd best stand up straight if you want her to believe you're strong enough to fight in her battle pit. Otherwise they'll have to shoot you with a crossbow.

"Look like you can be entertaining in the pit and you'll live for at least another day," they tell you.

The master approaches. Her beautiful body is clothed only in cryptic tattoos and tribal markings. She looks like a tropical fish. But her eyes are the same.

"Oh dear," Julia says when she sees you. "You're my slave?"

"So . . . you lived," you say.

"No thanks to you," she says.

You explain through the bars of your cage that you only left her at the mercy of her kidnappers because you could portend the Great Darkness of 2017, and you didn't see any point in helping her to live just so she could suffer the earth's pitiful demise.

"But here you are, with your own gasoline farm and everything," you say. "Looks like you came through okay."

"You, not so much," she says. Then she looks you over. "He'll fight tonight," she tells her guards. They nod and kneel before her. Just for fun, she grabs the crossbow from one of her guards and shoots the other in the face.

"It's important to make them think every day could be their last," she says to you. "Really makes life important. That's something I learned during my little bout of captivity back when gasoline flowed like water and the sky only turned bloodred at sunset."

At dusk, you're led from your cage and thrown into the pit of an amphitheater where Julia and her many soldiers and male concubines cheer as you do battle against two men who turned crisp in the Firestorm of 2020. They club you to death and then everyone eats a boar.

THE END

Shit Blows Up

When you get back to your car, there's a note on your windshield.

THERE IS NO PAST, it says.

You fold the note back up, then you're slammed against your car by the force of the fireball exploding outside of Deke's Surveillance. When you look up, his office has been obliterated. Someone shut him up, you think.

You race home, terrified about missing this mystery man's call, but doubly terrified of receiving it. When you burst into your apartment, Julia is there, sitting on your couch, looking utterly bewildered.

"How did you . . ."

She sees you, and in an instant she's off the couch and shoving you out your door. You get down to your car just in time to see your apartment explode in flames.

There's another note on your windshield. NO TRACE, it reads.

You and Julia drive off. She explains that the man who kept her captive was sheathed in darkness at all times and she has no idea who he is. "He's obsessed with you," she says.

"Why me?" you ask.

"I don't know," she says. "He liked to call you his brother, but he talked about you like you were a myth. 'The man who lives without living, who does everything he can not to leave a mark on the world.' He says you let him down, that you had your chances and you blew them all. He said he's going to make it so that *every* choice you make

from here on in results in the same blank fate, since that
is what you wish."

You don't know whether to trust Julia or whether she's
just a spy sent by the man who's been watching you.
Presently, though, there's no time to distrust her.

You take Julia to her place and she packs some things.
Back at the car, there's another note. EVERY TIME YOU LEAVE
A PLACE, I'M GONNA BLOW IT UP. GET THE PICTURE YET? it
reads. Then Julia's apartment blows up.

"He's taking all choice away from me," you say. "No
matter what I do or where I go, everything will just be reduced to smithereens in my wake. It's like I'll have never
existed."

You and Julia take to the road. You only enter buildings
when it is absolutely necessary, after hours, when no one is
there, since they will explode the minute you leave. This
forces you to become outlaws, breaking into stores and gas
stations. Julia never leaves your side for fear of being in
your trail and burned in the fire. The police arrest you on
occasion, but you're always able to escape when whatever
building you were just in explodes behind them and they
start shooting at the fire. Eventually, after many years, you
and Julia decide to call it quits.

"I love you," you tell her. "You are the only witness to
my having lived these many years. But I can't condemn
you to my fate. It's me he wants."

You take Julia to a dock and she gets on a boat headed
overseas, so she'll be sure never to step inside a place
where you just left. You wave good-bye, then you continue
down your lonely path across the earth, leaving everything
behind you in rubble. Eventually, the dull agony of knowing

that nothing that has known your presence can ever flourish grows too great to bear. Until one day, you go to a park late at night and step inside the men's room. Once you're sure no one is there, you step outside, then you dive back through the door just in time to be swallowed in a burst of flames.

THE END

Makin' Out on the Lunch Counter

You spend your shift at Lunch Counter delivering the customers their ground veal sloppy joe platters while trying to convince yourself that you've done the right thing and that you have to keep yourself open to possible opportunities. To distract yourself, you start coming on to Marie, the waitress you wanted to sleep with the entire time you were with Kim.

"Busy night, huh, Marie?" you say with a great deal of seduction in your voice. Marie won't answer before she is grabbed from behind by a soldier in uniform. He's Marie's boyfriend just back from the war. She wanted to get married before he got shipped out, but he wasn't so sure.

"MARIE!" he shouts.

"Johnny!" she replies.

"When I left I thought I was gonna live forever," Johnny says. "Instead I spent the last two years praying I'd live long enough to lay you down across this lunch counter and make something happen."

"Right here in front of everybody?" she asks.

The customers have gone silent. They watch the reunited lovers, eager.

"Right here in front of everybody," Johnny says.

The customers pull their plates and the salt and pepper shakers out of Marie and Johnny's way, and then they wait.

"Oh, Johnny," Marie says.

Johnny picks Marie up, lays her down on the lunch

counter, climbs on top of her, and the two of them make out. When Johnny puts his hand on Marie's right breast, the customers burst into applause. A little bit of this war just got won by the good guys.

If you want to be so inspired by the act of a soldier coming home for his woman that you quit right then and there to go save Julia, go to page 106.

If you wanna just watch them make out, go to page 13.

Child of a Broken Home

Your parents announced their decision to divorce a month ago, and visits home have been hell ever since. They eat lunch silently, attempting a semblance of civility for your benefit, until one of them inevitably erupts at a thinly veiled insult and storms from the table. At least today you have something to send the conversation down a different path.

"I need fifty thousand dollars," you say.

Your mother drops her cutlery onto her plate. Your father keeps chewing.

"This for a girl?" he asks through his mouthful of tuna salad.

"Yeah," you say. "She's been kidnapped. They're gonna kill her."

"Why haven't we heard about this girl if it's so serious?" your mother asks.

"It's not serious!" That came out louder than you'd intended.

"Fifty thousand dollars sounds pretty serious to me," your mother says.

"Will you leave him alone?" your father says. "Sooo, she pretty?"

Your mother jumps up from the table. "I am trying to be a mother to him. You're just trying to score points."

Your father stands up to meet her stare. "I am trying to help him to live his life without being tainted by all the shit you're putting him through."

"What *I'm* putting him through?" She looks like she's about to cry for a second. But she swallows her sobs and her eyes freeze over. "You black-hearted little man. Go on, give your son fifty thousand dollars to blow on some girl he barely knows. You always rescue him before he has a chance to try to do anything on his own. That's why he's already thirty-three and amounted to so little."

To you she says, "Sorry about that."

"No problem," you say. Your mom has been making it clear to you since you were twenty-five that she is completely and utterly disappointed in you. You got used to it after not too long.

"He can't be making a bigger mistake with this girl than I made by marrying such a miserable bore," your mother shouts as she runs from the table.

Your father yells at her back, "Hey, you owe the kid. Getting pregnant with him got me to marry you didn't it?!"

Your father sits back down. "Sorry about that," he says.

"No problem." You were nine when you first learned that your conception forced your parents into marriage, and you long ago came to grips with this knowledge.

Your dad drops his knife and fork on the plate. "This divorce must be hard on you, but it's for the best. She just can't get it out of her head that she could have done better than me. Of course she could have! So could I, if I'd bothered, but it doesn't keep me up at night. With her, though, it really pisses her off. Like there's someone in particular she thinks she missed her chance on."

"So can I have the fifty thousand dollars?"

"Lemme write you a check." He takes out his checkbook and begins scribbling.

If you want to sit down and think things through while watching the latest Zach Braff movie, go to page 5.

If you want to call in sick to your restaurant job so you can stay home and wait for the kidnappers to call, go to page 11.

They Always Go Back to Their Exes

After cashing your father's check, you go home and wait. When the phone rings at midnight, you're ready. You've got a pen and paper in front of you. You've got a stack of money at the ready in case he needs to hear you ruffle the bills into the phone. And you've got your resolve, which has never been stronger. Unlike every other project you've undertaken in your life, you will follow this thing through to the end.

"Never mind," the kidnapper says when he calls at midnight. "She wants to call her ex-boyfriend and have him handle the ransom."

"Ex-boyfriend?" you ask. "She never mentioned any ex-boyfriend to me."

They met three and a half years ago while she was finishing her master's in journalism at Northwestern. She wanted to move here right away after graduation, but he wanted to keep his ad job in Chicago. So she waited, putting her own career on hold for three years. When they finally moved here together, she broke it off a month after they arrived.

"But I was all ready to do this!" you complain to the kidnapper. "This was going to be the thing I came through on!"

"I guess when she called you and asked you to get that fifty grand, it was just kind of a . . . like a rebound thing," he says. "Oh wait, she wants to talk."

The phone changes hands.

"It wasn't a rebound thing!" Julia says.

"Feels like a rebound thing," you sulk.

Julia sounds desperate. "I never wanted to see Leon again!" she says. "That's why I called you. I wasted so much time being with him, it needed to be a clean break."

"But now you want him back," you say.

"I could die down here," she says. "If this ransom thing gets screwed up or the police get involved, I'll be killed. I can't trust it to someone I barely know. Leon may be wrong for me, but he loved me, and he won't let me die."

"You think I'll let you die?" you ask.

"I don't know," she says. "I wanted to find out. I wanted to spend time with you and learn who you are because I liked you. You remind me of myself, which isn't too big a compliment."

You feel butterflies in your stomach, the way you do when you talk to someone for the first time after you realize you're falling for them. You can hear the smile in her voice.

"But true to form, just when it looked like I was finally going to take control of my life, I went and got kidnapped," she says. "Now I have to call Leon and I'll owe him this big debt and I just know we'll end up back together."

"How do you know Leon will even pull this off?" you ask.

"Because Leon pulls stuff off," she says. "It's sickening."

"You don't have to go back to him," you say.

"And I didn't have to stay with him for the past three and a half years, but I did anyway," she says. "I tend to make choices that put a big delay on my life. Grad school. Leon. If you knew me you might suspect that I requested this kidnapping."

You really are falling for her now. "Let me just try," you say.

"Hopefully I'll see you when I'm free. Maybe I'll even cheat on Leon with you if you're up for it," she says with a laugh. "But right now, I have to do whatever ensures that I'll get out of this alive."

The phone changes hands.

"You know what sucks about being a kidnapper?" the kidnapper asks you.

"I don't know," you say. "The bureaucracy?"

"What sucks is," he continues, "when you burst in and yank someone out of her life, you never know what kind of fragile shit she was trying to hold together that's just gonna fall all to pieces thanks to you. It's harder to live with this kind of thing on my conscience than with the ones I end up killing."

The kidnapper hangs up and you sit staring at the phone, wondering what it would have been like if you had met Julia six months from now, after she'd already been rescued by Leon and they got back together and enough time had passed that she was ready to try and break it off with him again. It might have been really perfect.

If you want to wait until six months from now, after she's already been rescued by Leon and she's gotten back together with him and enough time has passed that she might be ready to try to break it off with him again, go to page 40.

If you want to go off and try to rescue her anyway because you're just so damn smitten with her that you can't let her slip away, go to page 9.

The Ghost of Your Dead Best Friend Has Some Career Advice

Your dead best friend Lenny has something he wants to say to you. Lenny was your best friend from middle school through the beginning of high school. He used to tell you how he wanted to be an Olympic diver, and you used to tell him how you wanted to be a world-famous actor. Lenny was as good at diving as you are at acting, which is why he's dead now. He cracked his head open after jumping from a thirty-foot cliff into the swimming hole at the bottom of the old quarry where you used to swim. You dragged him from the water and held him in your arms as he took his last breaths.

"Live your dream for both of us," he rasped. "Never give up on acting."

You've always remembered Lenny's dying words. He is one of the reasons you've managed to stick it out all of these years, despite the constant rejection and seemingly limitless discouragement. No matter how hard it gets, you're always able to buckle down and keep going. For Lenny.

Just before you make your decision about whether you want to give up on acting so that you can save Julia's life, a cold wind comes blowing through the room. Your vision seems to go black except for a bright white tunnel of light, from which the translucent image of Lenny floats toward you. He is the same age that he was on the day he died, except there is no wound where he hit his head. Also, he's naked.

"Lenny?" you ask the spirit.

"It is me," he says. "Your friend. Do not be afraid to look upon me. You need not avert your eyes."

"I'm not afraid. It's just that you're naked," you say. "And you still look fifteen. It's kind of uncomfortable to look at a naked fifteen-year-old boy."

"I come to you as I was on the day that I died," he says.

"You were naked when you died?" you ask.

"We both were," he says.

"We used to swim naked?" you ask. "Really?"

"Really," he says. "Those summer days swimming naked with you are the fondest memories of my corporeal life."

"It was great swimming with you," you say. "I must have just blotted the naked part out."

"It's understandable, old friend," Lenny says. "Now, then, I come to you today to tell you something that is of the greatest import."

"Are you sure it wasn't just you who was naked?" you ask.

Lenny's ghost takes a deep breath. He is growing impatient. "It really isn't what I wanted to talk about. But yes, I'm sure. What I need to tell you is—"

"It's just that the memory of my best friend dying in my arms," you say, interrupting, "and me begging you not to go, to hold on and be strong for me, and me kissing your forehead and crying into your hair—it's the most vivid memory from my childhood. I just think us both being naked at the time would be a detail that I wouldn't forget."

Lenny takes another deep breath. You're not sure, since he's floating, but it looks like he might be tapping his foot impatiently.

"Okay," he says. "If it's such a vivid memory, what color swimsuit were you wearing?"

You think for a second. Nothing comes. "Holy shit!" you shout. "We used to swim naked!"

"Yes, quite a surprise, I'm sure," Lenny says. "Anyway, I've come here today all the way from the afterlife, which is not a short trek, to tell you it's perfectly fine if you give up on acting."

You feel like he just punched you in the ribs. "But your dying words!" you say.

"I know what I said, but we were children at the time," Lenny says. "Since then I've kept tabs on your career and, well, I think if you turn your back on acting, the craft will survive."

"All these years," you say. "It was your dying wish that kept me going."

"Oh, please," Lenny shouts, causing his sparsely haired scrotum to rise and tighten. "You used my dying wish as an excuse. You've been stuck at the same place for over a decade, going on pointless auditions that were open to anyone with a copy of *Back Stage,* while just barely pursuing workshops or theater collectives that might help you develop. Any time the idea of going into some other field presented itself, you'd use my dying wish as an excuse to avoid making a scary decision about your life."

You're sulking now. "You don't think I'll make it?"

"I know you won't make it. You were supposed to figure it out on your own about three years from now, but there's a girl's life at stake, and believe me, you giving it a go for a little while longer is so not worth a girl losing her life."

"But Lenny . . ." you say.

Lenny starts to float back up the tunnel of white. "Give up on acting. Save the girl and eventually go to grad school," he calls out. "Oh, and by the way," he adds, "we once watched each other jerk off. Behind your parents' garage."

"I remember that, Lenny," you shout, waving good-bye to your old friend, your eyes filling with tears. "Of course I could never forget that day, old friend. And forget it I never will."

If you want to take Lenny's advice and give up on acting so you can save the girl, go to page 65.

If on second thought you decide to go in to work because you figure maybe Lenny is just trying to make you give up because he's jealous that you got to live on and become a man while he died in a quarry full of stagnant water, go to page 171.

There's Always Time
for Breakup Sex

When you hang up the phone, you hear a key in the lock. You'd almost forgotten that Kim, your ex-girlfriend, had scheduled today to come by and pick up the bag of her stuff that she'd left behind. You weren't supposed to be here.

"Oh, for God's sake," Kim says when she sees you.

"I'm sorry. I got held up." You're still in bed. Under the sheets, you're naked.

"How did you get held up from getting the fuck out of bed and leaving the apartment?" she asks. She looks good. "That was all you had to do."

"The phone rang. This girl I—"

"Don't. Just tell me where the bag is."

You point to the kitchen. She's wearing her silver skirt, the one that's made of nothing at all, and a black tank top underneath her soft brown cardigan. You've never seen the cardigan before, but you've removed the tank top with your fingertips.

"How's your new place?" you shout over to her. She's looking in the refrigerator.

"Who's the girl?" she responds.

"What?"

"The girl who called you." She's standing in the doorway drinking a glass of juice. You look down to see if your erection is detectable from underneath the sheets. It isn't.

"No, she didn't call me. She was kidnapped. I have to—"

She slams her glass on the desk. "Jesus Christ, were you seeing her while we were together?"

"No," you say. "We went on one date together."

"And you're saving her from kidnappers?"

"She's new in town," you say with a shrug. "Sit with me."

Kim doesn't say anything for a second. Then, "Did you ever cheat on me?"

"No," you say. You look her in the eye. "I promise."

She sits on the edge of the bed. You don't move. She says, "I don't believe you. You know that, right? Tell me you know that I think you cheated on me. I need you to know that."

You nod. "I know it. I didn't cheat on you, but I know you think I did." You put your hand on her thigh and slide your fingers up underneath her skirt. She closes her eyes, removes her sweater and her tank top, then climbs on top of you.

The sex is the best the two of you have had in a long while, maybe better than when you first started going out. Afterward, she crawls off of you without so much as a peck on the lips and begins to dress.

"You're just gonna leave?" you ask.

She laughs. "Why? Do you want me to stay?"

In that instant, yes, you want her to stay. But she's not asking about that instant. You keep quiet.

When she's fully dressed, she picks up her bag and stands at the foot of the bed. "Go save your girlfriend," she says. Then she walks out the front door.

You mutter aloud to the furniture, "She's not my girl-friend."

If you want to ask your Web millionaire friend to loan you the ransom money, go to page 18.

If you want to unplug your phone and get really, really drunk, go to page 102.

Keep Coming Back—
It Sometimes Works!

When the Lotto numbers are drawn, you hit four numbers on three different tickets, each paying out $575. Julia's body is found the following evening, and Mia Mendoza does a follow-up story, splicing your interview in with footage of the police wheeling the body on a gurney out of an abandoned ketchup factory.

The next morning, Jay from Gamblers Anonymous tracks you down at your apartment and invites you to attend a Gamblers Anonymous meeting. He says your story would go over really well, and he'd be happy to be your sponsor.

You go to a meeting and become an instant hit. Everyone clamors to pull you into group hugs, pleading with you to forgive yourself and insisting that gambling is a disease so you don't have to take responsibility for anything shitty you've ever done.

Eventually, though, as you keep coming back, they get sick of you telling the same old story. They want some new material, and when you don't have any, they start to suspect that you aren't actually addicted to gambling.

Until one night, when you show up to a meeting, you're stopped at the front door and told you can't come in.

"But I let a girl die so that I could play the Lotto!" you argue. "I need to forgive myself."

"Gamblers Anonymous isn't just for people who do something shitty *while* gambling," Jay says. "You have to do something shitty because you think gambling's really awesome. Sorry, but this isn't for you."

"Then how am I supposed to deal with what I've done?" you ask.

"The only way gamblers know how to cope is by going into GA or jumping off a roof," he said. "I'm afraid GA is out for you, but if you wanna use the roof, we have roof access."

You say that that sounds fine. Jay leads you through the meeting to the stairs in the back. As you pass the rows of gamblers, they start heckling you with shouts of "Fraud!" and "Liar!" and "You're good with money!"

On the roof, you and Jay stand twenty feet from the edge, your shirt collar clenched in his fist. A few of the other recovering gamblers stand just paces behind you, waiting to watch you die.

"It'll happen fast," Jay says into your ear. "Like the spin of a roulette wheel, you'll only have a few seconds to get your chips where you want them, so if you have anything you want to say, say it now."

"There's no such thing as a hot streak," you say. "It's all random."

That pisses them all off. The end of your life begins with the force of Jay's fist on the back of your neck. He doesn't break stride as he rushes you across the roof and over the edge. Before you even hit the ground, they've already managed to forgive themselves for your death. *We wouldn't even be here if we didn't love the shit out of gambling the way we do,* they think.

Meanwhile, you spend your last few seconds of life falling, with Julia's death weighing heavily on your conscience. In the instant before you land, you wonder whether you'll see Julia in the afterlife. You hope you do, so that maybe you'll get the chance to apologize and make it up to her by taking her out for a second date.

THE END

The Grass Is Always Greener.
Always!

It is quite a surprise when Reggie, the evening guard, starts coming on to you. You've learned so little about your captors over the years, it's disorienting to suddenly discover that this man who has kept himself hidden under a black hood has been harboring a crush on you all this time. He has barely even spoken to you until today.

"Congratulations on the joyous news of your wedding," Reggie says to you when he comes in to collect your lunch trays. Julia is napping, so he keeps his voice to a whisper.

"Thanks," you say from the easy chair.

"It is wondrous," Reggie goes on, "to see love blossom where one least expects it. It stands as proof that love will not be denied, no matter the obstacles. Love will not suffer our excuses for why we could not possibly accept its embrace. Love has heard them all and it has met every single one with a disinterested yawn."

Reggie stands above you holding the trays, looking down at you through the eyeholes in his hood. You just barely make out the whites of his eyes, but you can see happiness there, as if he is elated simply to behold you.

"But she is my student and I am her professor, it would scandalize the campus!" Reggie says with mockery in his voice. "But we are of different races, the whispers in the neighborhood would be deafening! But I have already agreed to marry someone else, how could I ever rescind my word?!"

Reggie leans closer to you.

"But I am his captor, and he is my captive."

A silence follows. Reggie holds his posture in front of you, bent just a bit at his waist, the trays held before him. You are startled when Julia murmurs in her sleep. You look to her and make sure she hasn't woken, already feeling as if you've betrayed her.

Though your homosexual experiences have been limited only to several drunken encounters in college and the one time you jerked off in front of your best friend in high school, four years spent in captivity has changed your capacity to feel affection for another person, woman or man. These past years your world has been only a measure larger than a goldfish bowl, your social interaction limited to one woman and four men in hoods. You've learned every detail and nuance of this woman's being, and you have hardly a clue about the men. Yet this woman is now demanding that you promise the entirety of yourself to her. She is demanding that you shrink the fishbowl even farther. In contrast, this man before you is offering an entire realm of experience that you cannot even imagine, not until this minute as he bends slightly toward you at the waist, and shows you his parted pink lips through the mouth hole of his hood.

"I can hold my gun to your head if you want," he says. "So it'll look like you didn't have a choice."

If you want to choose to love Reggie, go to page 34.

If you want to remain committed to Julia, go to page 152.

Really Gross Sky Rockets in Really Disgusting Flight

With all the demands that have been put on you today, a fleeting encounter with a stranger is just too irresponsible for you to pass up. So you join her on the bench and the two of you have sex through your zippers. You're startled by how easy it is to ignore the monotonous grunting of the couple sharing the bench with you. You're not as startled by how appropriate your coupling feels. This is the level of intimacy that you deserve.

Just as you finish, before you can even pull up your zipper, the police swarm in and raid the rest area. You try to explain that you have to save a girl from kidnappers, but you can't be heard over the others as they shout about their children who won't be picked up from day care and the jobs they'll lose because they only have an hour for lunch. You're all thrown in the back of a police van and driven to jail.

You use your one phone call to call your voice mail and change your outgoing message remotely. The message you leave is as follows:

> *You have reached [your name and phone number]. I cannot come to the phone right now because I am in jail. If this is the kidnappers, tell Julia I'm sorry. Had she known me a little better, she would have known that I'm not the type of guy to save the day. I'm the type of guy who gets arrested for public indecency after he gets caught*

having sex with a stranger at a highway rest stop in the middle of the afternoon. I hope you can find someone else to get you that ransom money. Everyone else, please leave a message at the beep.

When you return to your cell, you find that several of the people from the rest stop have broken out into a group grope in the jail cell, so you ask if you can join in and they shift their weight to make space for you. It's warm in the group grope.

THE END

Special thanks to Ritch Duncan for running the beginnings of this book in the late, great *Jest Magazine*. And thanks to Byrd, Peter, and John. And, of course, to Amanda. Thank you.

Coming Soon...
Just Make a Choice! Book Two

The TERRIBLE HORRIBLE TEMP-to-PERM DEBACLE!

a *Just Make a Choice!* adventure
by **Bob Powers**

A Note on Being in Your Thirties and Not Having Amounted to Very Much at All

In this book, you're a THIRTY-THREE-YEAR-OLD ALCO-HOLIC TEMP with a dream of one day being a celebrated novelist. You've been asked to GO PERM at your temp job, but you worry that if you take a permanent job and get used to the benefits, like health insurance and paid holidays and team-building retreats, you'll GIVE UP ON YOUR DREAMS and spend the rest of your life wearing CORPORATE DRESS. The way you see it, you are far from the man you want to be, and at thirty-three, you know TIME IS RUNNING OUT. You don't want to make anything about your present life permanent, least of all your employment situation. As long as you KEEP EVERYTHING TEMPORARY, the sky's the limit.

Unfortunately, YOU DRINK TOO MUCH! When you wake up from a blackout with no memory of what happened the night before, you discover you've been FRAMED for murder. Someone wants you to take that permanent job, and he's ready to blackmail you into doing it. The ensuing adventure will force you to make a series of choices that not only will determine whether you spend the rest of your life IN PRISON or in A CUBICLE, but will also force you to ADD FOCUS to your career and your love life in ways that you've been avoiding ever since you got out of college.

BE VERY CAREFUL! You're DIRECTING THE STORY and the CHOICES you make can result in MURDER, DRY HEAVING, AMPUTATION, SHITTY HEALTH COVERAGE WITH A HIGH CO-PAY, SEXUAL HARRASSMENT, INTERNET PORN STAR-DOM, even DOCKERS PURCHASES! It's YOUR STORY and YOUR LIFE. All you've got to do is decide which page you want to turn to. *JUST MAKE A CHOICE!*

Wake Up, Temporary

You wake up naked, in a strange room, next to a strange girl. You have no idea where you are and no memory of how you got there. The only thing you recognize is the top of the Chrysler Building out the window. You're still in New York City. At least you didn't cross state lines like you did on your last bender.

Your cell phone is ringing. You find your pants on the floor by the bed and you fish the phone out of your pocket.

"Hello?"

"Why, you little shit! Get your ass to work right the fuck now or I'll find you wherever you are and rip your asshole out your mouth, you fucker!"

It's Holly, from your temp agency.

"Sorry, Holly. How late am I?" you ask.

"Late enough for me to get a phone call from their HR office looking for you. Plus, they're asking me what you've decided about going perm and I have to tell them I don't have a clue. Do you know how humiliating it is as a temporary employment services agent to admit that my own temps keep secrets from me? Let me in, dammit!"

It's coming back to you now. Today is the day you're supposed to go into your temp job at SkoolKidz, the nation's largest children's school uniform designer and manufacturer, and tell them whether you want to go perm as executive assistant to the CEO and founder, Ms. Haviland Payne. Last night you were mulling over the decision and the pressure all started to bear down on you, so you went to the bar underneath your apartment to have a drink. That's the last thing you remember.

"Well?" Holly barks. "Do you wanna go perm or not? Or do you still feel the need to build walls between us and keep me in the dark?"

Your mouth feels like you swallowed an old glue trap. You're so hungover that your vision is actually blurry and a little gray, as if you might faint before you even get out of bed. You're nauseous and you smell like cigarettes and buffalo wing sauce. Despite how cloudy and murky you feel, one thing remains perfectly clear.

"I can't go perm, Holly. I know it means a really big commission for you, but I just can't do it."

"Motherfucker!" she screams. You hear a crash on the other end. She probably threw a three-hole punch at somebody. "You been talking to Perky Temps?"

"No, I—"

"I know they've been calling you with assignments. Don't make me remind you that you are a member of the Tempting Temporaries family. And no one takes better care of you than your family. No one knows better how to destroy you, either."

"I'm not working with another agency. I just decided—"

"Well, decide again! Don't you want health insurance? You know what happens if you get hit by a car when you're uninsured? The ambulance just runs you over a bunch more times to put you out of your misery. You wanna die in the street?"

"No," you answer honestly.

"Oh, screw it, just get to work." Holly slams her phone down.

You drop the phone to the floor and it lands with a loud smack. You turn to the girl next to you to apologize for waking her, but she hasn't woken up. That's when you notice how wet the bed is.

Please please please don't let me be the one who peed, you think. You touch your hand to the soaking wet mattress and lift it up to your nose to—

Oh, shit. It's blood.

It's on your fingers. Now it's on the comforter. You peer under the sheets and find the mattress between you and the naked stranger is soaked in red. This isn't the first time you woke up from a blackout naked and covered in blood, but usually it's because you partied with the wrong kind of people, the kind who'll start the night fun and all "let's dance," and by the end of the night they're beating you senseless and stealing your clothes. This girl doesn't look like that kind of people.

She doesn't move when you shake her shoulder.

"Hey, you," you say. "You, on the bed."

She doesn't respond.

You roll out of bed, the panic making your heart race and aggravating your headache. You find some mail on her bureau. It's addressed to Laura Kennedy. Never heard of her.

You go around to her side of the bed and you finally get a look at her face. Even if you had met her before, you wonder if you would recognize her now. She looks to be made of stone. Her eyelids and lips are sealed so tight without a hint that her head ever contained any moving parts. You can see some blood on her neck, hinting at the throat wound just a half-inch down, thankfully hidden by the bedsheet. You run to the bathroom, ill.

Before you can make it to the toilet, you get a look in the mirror and you're frozen solid by what you see there. Scrawled in blood across the glass:

WELCOME TO THE WORLD OF
PERMANENT EMPLOYMENT!

What the shit happened last night?

You're sent running back into the bedroom when your phone rings again. The caller-ID screen reads "Unknown."

"Hello?"

"Who's ready to get himself some health insurance?" a man sings.

"Who the hell are you?" you ask.

"Who am I?" the man asks back. "Don't you have some more pressing questions? Such as, where the hell are you? What the hell happened last night? And who the hell is that dead girl in that gosh darn bed?" He's very jovial and it creeps you out. You'd prefer that he growl through a voice modulator or something.

"Who killed her?"

"Who killed the girl is a multiple-choice question. The answer is either, a) you. Or, b) not you. If you want to select b), go into SkoolKidz today and tell them you wanna go perm."

You're thrown. "Who the hell are you?" you ask again.

"An interested party. One who can make all evidence of everything that happened last night disappear. One who can also make a shitload of cops swarm that apartment like locusts in under five minutes. Depending on whether or not you decide to accept permanent employment."

"And if I don't?"

"You go to jail for capital murder."

"So I either have to accept a permanent position as an executive assistant in an office environment that requires corporate dress, or I spend my life in prison?"

"That's pretty much it. What's it gonna be, Temporary?"

If you wanna just go to the police and turn yourself in right now, turn to page 204.

If you want to try to clean up the scene of the crime and dispose of the body, turn to page 207.

They Don't Make You
Sing "Happy Birthday"
to People in Jail

You've watched enough police procedural shows on TV to know that you couldn't possibly clean that apartment of all of your clothing fibers, fingerprints, DNA, and, you're betting, semen. With no memory of what happened last night, you have no way of defending yourself should the police come calling. The man on the phone promised that he would make this all go away only if you agree to take the permanent position at your office job. Since that's too nightmarish even to think about, you're just going to have to turn yourself in to the police and hope that because you're cooperating they only give you life in prison instead of the chair.

As you ride the elevator down, you're surprised by just how relieved you feel. Yes, you're on your way to confess to a murder you might not have committed, but all that means to you is you don't have to go into work today. You don't have to decide whether to accept your executive assistant position permanently or go on temping further into your thirties. You don't have to disappoint your girlfriend anymore (she's been very patient). You don't have to worry about the future because with one night of extremely irresponsible behavior, your future has been made crystal clear. You only have one thing to do, and that's die in jail.

The elevator doors open and the doorman is standing in the lobby as if he were waiting for you. He's in his sixties, with a large belly, and he looks very unhappy. "You got a lotta nerve showing your face around here after last night," he says.

You consider just making a run for it. You want to go to the police yourself before someone else reports the murder. It will be worse for you if they're made to come and get you.

"You had a good time in Ms. Kennedy's apartment, then? Throw a nice party, did you? I guess you lingered about so that you could humiliate me some more?"

You note that the doorman stinks of urine.

"I'm just a working man, son," he says. "I been opening doors for forty-five years so that I could make a nice life for my family. Not so that party boys like you can phone down and send me out to the sidewalk to hail a cab, unaware that you're on the roof waiting to drop a balloon full of your own waste on my head."

Oh dear Lord, what happened last night?

"I'm sorry," you say.

"He's sorry! Oh, so you are capable of being a man," he says. "You were certainly playing the innocent little lamb last night when I knocked on Ms. Kennedy's door. You're lucky Laura Kennedy takes good care of me with her Christmas envelope or you can be sure the police would have paid you a visit. So is everyone out of that apartment or do I have to see more of you then?"

"Everyone?" you say. "There were others?"

"There better have been with the racket you all were making. What of that other girl who answered the door? The one who was wearing the painters' coveralls and rubber gloves? She's the only one who seemed to have her wits about her."

"Rubber gloves? Tell me what she looked like. Tell me."

The doorman shakes his head. "You keep drinking like that, son, and you're not going to have much brain left after too long. Now get going or else I will call the cops."

You leave the building and start walking. So someone else was there last night. Maybe even more than one person. If you can find that girl, she might be able to prove that you didn't do it. Of course, she might also be the killer, in which case she might not like you tracking her down. Regardless, finding someone else who was in that apartment last night will only get you closer to the truth.

You turn the corner and find yourself down the block from a police precinct.

If you think that hunting for the girl in the painters' coveralls and rubber gloves is way too much effort and you just want to go ahead and confess to the murder without bothering, turn to page 210.

If you want to go grab a drink and think this through, turn to page 213.

You Always Were Kind
of a Neat Freak

You've watched so many police procedural shows on TV that by now you know exactly how to clean that apartment of any evidence that could connect you to the murder. You just have to rid the space of all hair follicles, clothing fibers, fingerprints, footprints, personal belongings, and traces of microscopic DNA you might have left behind. It's a bit involved, but far preferable to going perm at your day job.

Also, be sure to gather up any diaries or journals in the apartment. Even though this woman is a stranger to you, you might not have been a stranger to her. She might have secretly loved you from afar for years and yesterday she might have finally had the gumption to introduce herself to you and take you home. In which case, you'd probably be all over her diary, and the entry written on the night she died would probably read something like, "Dear Diary, no more pining away. Tonight I'm just going to walk right up to [YOUR NAME] and tell him he can take me home and do whatever he wants to me. If anyone comes looking for me, Diary, tell them to go and hunt down [YOUR NAME], because as of two hours from now, my fate is entirely in his hands. Bet on it, Diary." So yeah, no diaries.

Of course, most important of all is the semen. One microscopic drop of seminal fluid can tell a forensics expert that when you were in the fourth grade you did a book report on *A Wrinkle in Time* and got a C. No matter how long it takes or how many blacklight bulbs you have to burn through, get rid of any and all semen that you can find. Don't worry about if it's yours or someone else's. If it's semen, it's leavin'.

You start scrubbing away at the blood on the mirror but it isn't too long before you run out of absorbent sponges. So you head down to the corner deli to stock up on supplies. While you're there you order yourself a bacon, egg, and cheese sandwich on a bagel. The guy behind the sandwich counter doesn't move, so you repeat yourself.

"Bacon, egg, and cheese on an everything bagel," you tell him.

The sandwich maker just glowers at you.

"Is there a problem?" you ask.

"You got a lotta nerve showing your face in here again," the sandwich maker says.

That's when you notice all of the little laminated signs on the deli case detailing the deli's various sandwich specials, such as "The Fifth Avenue" and "The Bobby De Niro." Someone apparently scribbled on all of the signs with a red Sharpie. So the "Fifth Avenue" reads, "Swiss Cheese, Honey Ham, Dijon Mustard, *AND HOMO SAUCE*." The "Bobby De Niro" reads, "Prosciutto, Provolone Cheese, Sweet Peppers, *DICK BOOGERS,* Oil, and Vinegar."

You have to stifle a smile when you see that the "Cagney & Lacey" (turkey and brie cheese) now includes a helping of *"QUEEFONAISE."* But the sandwich maker is not laughing.

"I did this?" you ask.

"While I had my back turned making those twelve burgers you ordered and then walked out on. You're lucky your friend came in after to pay for the food and the signs, or else you'd be talking to the police right now."

"My friend?"

"Yeah, I couldn't believe you had any, either," he says. "Well-dressed guy. Classy. Kind of overly happy when he talked in a way that creeped me out a little. Paid me a little extra to keep it to myself that I had even seen you in the store in case any cops came by. You still want that egg sandwich?"

"You're gonna do something gross to it, aren't you?"

"I'm afraid I have no choice, yes."

"Just the sponges."

It had to be the man on the phone who paid off the deli guy. He must have been in control of your entire night, watching you every step of the way. Even if you get rid of all evidence, chances are this guy will be able to pin the murder on you anyway. You need to find out who he is and what he wants with you. The only way to do that, unfortunately, is to go into the office and go perm.

If you want to go into the office and go perm, turn to page 217.

If you want to just get the hell out of town and spend the rest of your life in hiding, turn to page 220.

This Could Be Your
In Cold Blood!

As you approach the police station, your belly is churning not with dread, but with excitement. You know that if you go to jail for a crime you (probably) didn't commit, you've got a great big bestseller of a book on your hands. It breaks your heart to shelve your novel in progress about a group of thirty-year-olds who find love and wisdom while helping distribute bottled water to Katrina refugees. That story needs to be told, certainly, but you honestly haven't made much progress lately. A meaty nonfiction side project about your own wrongful imprisonment might be just the distraction you need to get back on track. Top it off with the ambiguity of a narrator who has no memory of the night in question, and you've got a thriller on your hands. It'll be like *The Bourne Identity* if Jason Bourne were an alcoholic temp.

Sure, you might not get rich since convicts aren't allowed to profit from selling their stories, but you won't need money in jail. Cigarettes, blow jobs, and shivvings; that's the currency "inside." Money is no concern because you can feel in your gut that this is the book you were born to write. This is the book that will finally transform you from aging temporary office assistant to bestselling author. You can't even wait to get into the quiet solitude of that jail cell and starting putting crayon to toilet paper.

When you enter the station, you go to the desk sergeant and you tell him, "I'd like to turn myself in."

"What for?" the sergeant asks without looking up from his newspaper.

"Murder," you say.

The sergeant looks up at you, then shouts, "We got him!"

In what feels like a nanosecond, a cloud of policemen surrounds you and you're cuffed and planted on the ground with a knee on the back of your neck. They must have already found Laura Kennedy's body. They must have already been hunting you down. You can already see this moment taking shape in the opening paragraphs to your masterpiece. You can't help smile.

"You think this is funny, huh?" the officer who cuffed you says, noticing your smile. "You know, you got a lotta nerve showing your face in here again."

Again?

In the interrogation room, you learn that you were brought to that station last night after you climbed up on the hood of a parked squad car, exposed yourself to the officers inside, and proceeded to mash your genitals against the windshield in mock ecstasy. When you were brought into the station, you apparently threw up on the very desk sergeant to whom you just surrendered. He then threw up on one of the arresting officers, who threw up on the other arresting officer, who in turn threw up on a pair of detectives, and so on until nearly everyone in the station was either throwing up, being thrown up on, or slipping hilariously in puddles of throw up, allowing you to escape by staggering casually out the front door.

"Murder?" the officer interrogating you asks. His name is Officer Cortez and he doesn't seem very excited to hear your confession. "Who'd you kill?"

You tell him about Laura Kennedy and that he would find in her bed with her throat cut. Your prints are all over the apartment, you tell him. Your semen probably is, too.

"Probably?" the officer asks. "So, you don't remember whether or not you ejaculated last night? That kind of thing's usually hard to forget. Me, I can remember every single blast."

"I was blacked out," you say.

"Tell me," Cortez asks. "How'd you kill her? What kind of weapon?"

You tell him you don't remember. Cortez grabs your shirt lapels.

"Well, you listen to me, you little drunken reprobate," he barks in your face. "I got a guy two doors down who says he does remember. We picked him up for a murder six months old, and in the process of confessing he copped to the murder of Laura Kennedy and we make him for a whole bunch of other murders that we been scratching our heads over. Now I'm in support of anyone in your age group taking responsibility for himself, but I don't need any conflicting testimony from some alky coming off a bender. Keep your lips sealed, you hear me, Andy Capp? This ain't your show."

Officer Cortez refuses to believe your story, no matter how insistent you are. You end up being charged with misdemeanor disorderly conduct. They'd like to charge you with a felony for escaping police custody and assaulting an officer, but they would have to put on record that a drunk man had thwarted an entire police station using his own sick as a weapon. You're ordered to perform one hundred hours of community service and attend Alcoholics Anonymous.

You're not going to jail and you're not going to be a famous author. You're the same failed novelist/aging temp that you were yesterday, except now you have to admit to a drinking problem and spend your weekends picking up trash on roadsides.

If you want to try to write the story of the guy who went to jail for your crime, turn to page 223.

If you want to really throw yourself into the arms of recovery, turn to page 226.

Heaven Knows You're
Miserable Now

Your hangover is so bad that you're starting to hear voices, so you decide to head over to your favorite bar, Kilgarry's, owned by the brothers Sully and Tully Kilgarry. It's around the corner from the Transit Authority, so they open at 8 A.M. for all the transit employees coming off third shift. It's a good bet that you stopped in there last night, so they might be able to give you some helpful information.

When you reach Kilgarry's, it's gone. Burned to the ground. The only thing standing is the ornately carved oak bar, but it's blackened with ash. Tully is behind it with his head in his arms. He's crying. Sully is rubbing his back, trying to comfort him. You're afraid to approach them. Afraid to find out what you already know.

"Sully?" you say.

"You got a lotta nerve showing your face around here again," Sully shouts.

Yup, looks like you burned down your favorite bar. Sully and Tully are both very emotional as they berate you for the careless antics that reduced their family legacy to a square lot of cinders. Amidst all the swearing and crying you discern that apparently you got so drunk last night you started to hallucinate that you were in France during World War II, and that you didn't want the invading Nazis to get their hands on your country's supply of Coors Light, so you poured a bottle of 151-proof rum all over the upholstered booths and you set the place on fire. Then you took off your pants and shouted *"Viva la resistance!"* a bunch of times before coming out of the hallucination, putting your pants back on, and running to safety.

"Sorry," you say to them.

You're told to fuck off and you comply. You're beginning to

worry that you might never find out what went on last night, and that if you keep looking you'll only get more depressed as you discover all the people you've hurt and exposed your genitals to while in the midst of your blackout. You might have no choice but to do what the man on the phone said and go perm at your office job. But going perm feels like the final nail in the coffin for your dreams of finishing your novel and getting it published.

You just don't know what the hell to do next.

If you want to burst into a publisher's office and tell him that he absolutely has to read your novel right now because you're about to take a permanent job and give up on writing forever and he'll miss out on the chance to publish what might be the greatest American novel of our time, turn to page 215.

If you want to go to Kinko's and make some signs, turn to page 227.

Publish or Perish

You run home and grab your unfinished manuscript, then you sprint to Midtown. You race through the Random House lobby and you hop over the security gates, careful not to drop the box containing your manuscript, and you slip into an elevator just as the doors are closing. The security team phones the police, but they're too late. You're already in.

When your elevator doors open on the top floor, you sprint past the receptionist and take off down the hall for the publisher's office. He's in the middle of a meeting when you burst through his door.

"I'm sorry to interrupt, sir," you say. "But I'm an aspiring author and I need you to read my manuscript."

"Of course!" the publisher says. "Just leave it with my receptionist and I'll give it a read as soon as we finish up here."

"No!" you bark, spittle flying from your mouth. "You have to read it now! I'm about to go perm at my office job to avoid going to jail and if I do that, I'll give up writing forever. I just know I will. You have to read my book right this minute because for all you know, this could be the greatest novel of our time!"

The publisher looks around at the others in the room. "Guess I don't have a choice. Everybody out! I have to read this young man's novel."

You plop the pages on his desk and then you sit on the floor with your knees pulled to your chest while he reads for the next six hours. When he's done, he comes over and puts his hand on your shoulder.

"It's not that good," he says. "It could be good if you keep working on it."

"Really?" you say.

"It could also get worse," he says. "Depends, really."

"But I have to take a permanent office job and I'll probably never write again," you say.

"That's too bad. But I can't publish it the way it is, it not being good and all," he says. "Thanks for letting me read it, though. I love reading."

The publisher leads you to the elevator. When the doors open on the ground floor, you see the police across the lobby waiting for you. They're either after you for harassing the publisher, or because they found Laura Kennedy's body. Either way, you gotta start running.

If you want to run toward the bookstore down the block, PICK UP BOOK TWO AT A BOOKSTORE NEAR YOU!

If you want to run to your girlfriend for help, YOU'RE JUST GONNA HAVE TO WAIT. . . .

Welcome to the Rest
of Your Life

You march in and tell Haviland Payne that you'd like to accept her offer to come on permanently as her executive assistant.

"You've got a lot of nerve showing your face in here"—she pauses to take in your clothes—"in such slovenly dress."

"I'm sorry," you say. "I had a late night and overslept. I didn't want to blow my chance at this job, so I rushed right in without cleaning myself up."

Ms. Payne has her legs up on her desk. She reclines with the self-satisfaction that comes only with knowing that yours is the most powerful school uniform manufacturer in the country. Her skirt is very short and the hem is not visible above the desktop, so it looks like she's wearing nothing below the waist. You've encountered this vision nearly every day as her temp, usually around 3 P.M., and it always makes you focus your eyes elsewhere. Today you focus them on the building across the street. You keep your eyes on a window where you can see a man standing as still as a coatrack. Is he watching you?

"I thought you were worried about having enough time to write," she queries.

You don't answer right away. You can't take your eyes off the man in that distant window. You can't see anything but a shape. He could be staring at anything. His back could be turned for all you know. But you're sure that's the man who called you this morning. Perhaps paranoia is setting in, but you're certain that he's waiting to somehow confirm that you take the job. You'd better convince Ms. Payne that you really want this job. If she withdraws her offer, you could be arrested for murder before happy hour.

"I need to start being realistic," you murmur.

She doesn't seem convinced.

"I need to think about when I'm old," you try. "I don't want to get old without having saved."

Now she looks almost amused.

"I don't think I'll ever write anything that matters. I don't think I'll ever amount to anything." You say this with your full voice. You say it like it's the truth.

Haviland can tell you're shaken. She pulls her legs off the desk and crosses her arms on her desk pad. Her manner is gentler now, like she'd been playfully teasing a child who suddenly burst into tears.

"Of course, I'll be happy to have you come on permanently," she says. "But did something happen that influenced your decision?"

You're staring at the window again. The man is gone. Haviland turns to see what's out there.

"No, Ms. Payne," you say. "Just started taking stock, I guess."

If she doesn't let you go to your desk soon, she might see you cry.

"Well, welcome aboard. HR will be in contact with you soon."

You rush from her office and hide your head in your desk drawer to try to contain what feels like a dry heave coming on. You never spoke those words before. "I'll never write anything that matters." You never allowed yourself to entertain that thought as a real possibility, and now that you've said it to someone else you feel as if it's the only possibility. It's why you've made sure never to finish your book. You fear that working on it is the only proof that you're a writer.

You catch your breath and sit up straight, gripping your desk. You try to convince yourself that you were only saying what you thought she needed to hear, but you can't get over the feeling that you just officially gave up on your dream.

Just then someone drops an envelope on your desk. It reads, "Sarah's Wedding Donations!" Apparently someone in the office named Sarah is getting married and everyone's chipping in for a wedding gift. You've never gotten one of these envelopes before since the company mercifully has a policy against soliciting temporaries for donations for things like wedding gifts or Girl Scout cookies. You're not sure how much to give.

If you want to contribute ten dollars to Sarah's wedding envelope, PICK UP BOOK TWO AT A BOOKSTORE NEAR YOU!

If you want to contribute thirty dollars to Sarah's wedding envelope, YOU'RE JUST GONNA HAVE TO WAIT. . . .

Get Your Back Wet

You go to Canada and register with a temp agency in Toronto. The process is almost identical to the American agencies, except you have to remember during your typing test to spell almost every word with an added *U* thrown in someplace. Your Word and Excel scores are near perfect and Kat, your very pretty temp agent, is excited to get you started.

"I just need your identification," she says.

You show Kat your New York license and U.S. passport.

"Oh," she says. "You need Canadian citizenship to work up here. Which is great for me, actually."

"Why?" you ask, suddenly hopeless to be able to survive on the lam.

"Because I'm not allowed to date my temps. Can I buy you dinner?"

Kat takes you to a nice Canadian restaurant, where you have a delicious meal of moosemeat soup and fried woodchuck. Then she takes you to her apartment and you promptly move in.

Kat allows you to live rent-free while you work on your book. You love the idea of one day being able to say that part of your book was written in Canada. You imagine that printed on the last page: *New York and Toronto, 2002–2008. (Or 2009? 2010?)*

The first few months you sit down to write every morning, but you don't make it a half hour before you just start staring out the window and watching Canadians do stuff. Eventually you stop trying to work on the book altogether and Kat starts to get impatient.

"I'm a temp agent. I can't stand to see someone not working. It hurts me right here," she says, tapping on her chest. "If you're not working on your book, you should be finding some other way to work in this country. For example, you could marry me and gain citizenship."

"I'm just blocked right now, Kat," you say. "I need the freedom to pick it back up when I'm ready. I need the possibility that I'll be free to listen when my muse calls again, and if I take up steady work right now that possibility will be eliminated."

Kat takes a deep breath. She says, "I know it's not about the book, or about writing. It's about commitment, isn't it?"

You don't answer.

"I know why you're in Canada. I know what you're running from."

Your heart is pounding now. You try to appear calm.

"What do you mean?" you manage to ask.

She takes your hand in hers. "I know about the offer to go perm in New York. How you got scared of taking a permanent job so you fled the country. I spoke with Holly, your old temp agent—"

"You what?" you shout. You jump to your feet and check the front window.

"I was worried," she says. "I wasn't sure what I was getting myself into. So I keyed into GROTSD, the Global Repository of Temporary Staffing Data, and found your record with Holly at Tempting Temporaries in the U.S. She said you were a very valuable temp, often requested, and when you ran off on her instead of taking the job you and she had worked toward for years, it broke her heart."

You grab Kat's shirt. "When did you talk to her? How long ago?"

"Yesterday. Around eighteen hours ago."

"Pack your things," you say.

But you don't even get to leave the room before a blast takes the back door off its hinges and Holly walks in, brandishing a pistol.

"Thanks for finding my boy," she says to Kat. "I'm taking him home now."

"Please, Holly, it wasn't you or the job. It was something way bigger than that. I was being framed for—"

"Murder?" she says. "You damn fool. Don't you know to come to your temp agency with a problem like that? We have cleaners to scrub crime scenes so our temps can make it in to their assignments on time. We'd be run out of business if we had to send a temp on the lam every time he committed a capital offense."

"So the coast is clear?"

"It took a little extra effort since you didn't come to us first. We had to kidnap the DA's kid for a goddamn month before he'd pin the crime on some drifter. But yes, my little proletariat, the coast is clear. You ready to come home and work?"

"I can't go perm, Holly," you say. "I can't do it."

"You don't have to, sweetie," Holly says, pulling your head to her bosom. "That job was filled months ago. You can temp as long as you like and if you ever want to take the plunge, so be it. But I won't pressure you."

You stand up straight with a smile and Holly wipes the tears from your cheeks.

"I'll get my things," you say.

Kat steps in your way. "What about me?" she asks.

"I'm sorry, Kat," you say. "Thank you for all that you've given me. But Holly's my temp agent."

You look over your shoulder at Holly, smiling proudly back at you.

"And she always will be."

You pack your bag and get into Holly's car, and she drives you over the border. The minute you cross into the States a drunk driver plows into you. Since you don't have insurance, the ambulance takes Holly away and leaves you in the burning car. You fall out of the car and crawl your way back toward Canada and its free health care. You die just feet from the border. The border patrol lets you rot there until an American body disposal truck picks you up to dispose of your remains in a potter's field someplace in Buffalo.

THE END

You're Just Trying to Give Voice to the Voiceless for Fuck's Sake!

With no murder to be wrongly imprisoned for, you're feeling pretty hopeless. You had dreams of being heralded as "an important new voice shouting from the bowels of America's penal system," and with those dreams dashed, you know it will be impossible to go back and try to slog your way through your novel again. So you go into SkoolKidz and accept the permanent position as executive assistant to Haviland Payne.

"I thought you were worried about having enough time to write," Ms. Payne queries.

"That's when I thought I had something to write," you say.

"Wonderful. No dreams. My last assistant was trying to pursue her dream and she turned out to be a nightmare. I need someone like you, someone who doesn't want anything that he can't find in a Staples catalog."

Though you took the permanent job, the mysterious man who tried to set you up for the murder never contacts you. You assume that with someone having already confessed to the murder of Laura Kennedy, he no longer has any leverage and so he's forgotten about you.

For the first six months you give Ms. Payne exactly what she wants: consciousness, punctuality, and a lack of ambition that would be diagnosed as depression in any other environment. The only glimmer of hope you allow yourself is reading about the trial of Keith Fowler, the drifter who falsely confessed to the murder you were hoping to be falsely imprisoned for. Every day when you open the paper you pray to see a picture of Fowler with his long black hair and thick black beard growing from his pale white skin, underneath the headline, "New Evidence Casts Doubt on Killer's Confession!"

Unfortunately, your prayers are never answered. And one day you open up the paper and you see the word "Guilty!" You adjourn to a men's room stall and you weep.

Not long after Fowler's sentencing, you go in on a Saturday to finally begin your community service. You had put it off for a while but you're running out of time to complete those hundred hours by the end of the year. You show up at the clerk's office, where they give you an orange vest and drive you out to a highway to pick up garbage off the side of the road. That's when your luck changes.

There on the other side of the highway is Keith Fowler, along with a dozen other inmates clearing brush from the road's shoulder. You're compelled to make contact with the killer who has no knowledge of having murdered your dreams.

"Mr. Fowler!" you shout over the noise of the traffic. "Mr. Fowler, why'd you confess to the murder of Laura Kennedy?"

"Growing up, I was taught that if you do wrong, you oughta try to make up for it by doing right," Fowler shouts back from his side of the interstate. "What's one more count of murder if it means a bereaved family might be given some closure?"

The corrections officer blows his whistle and the inmates are hustled back in the truck. As you watch the truck pull away, Keith Fowler's words echo in your mind. You weren't meant to write a book about your own wrongful imprisonment, you realize. You were meant to write the Keith Fowler story.

The next Saturday you arrive at the highway ready to begin the research process. The corrections officer won't allow you to come to Fowler's side of the interstate, so you're forced to shout him questions from across the road and do your best to make out his answers while jotting down notes on a small pocket notebook.

The stuff that's shouted across that four-lane highway is pure bestseller gold. Fowler tells all about his life growing up in a shack in the plains of Texas, with his abusive father and sick mother with a heart of gold. He tells of the day his fate was sealed, when he robbed a candy shop in order to pay for his mama's medicine. He got the prescription to her and then he went on the lam, knowing the cops would be looking for him. From then on he led a life of violence, the kind of life his daddy taught him to lead. You keep showing up for community service long after you've fulfilled your sentence and after several hundred hours of shouting across a highway, you've got one hell of a book on your hands.

One day you show up to the highway and a man in a suit is waiting for you. He introduces himself as Mr. Fowler's agent and he hands you a cease and desist letter.

"We've already got the deal in place for Mr. Fowler's story," the agent tells you. "And we've contracted with the best ghostwriter in town. I'm sorry, but you'll have to find another gentle-hearted killer to exploit."

"Where am I going to find another subject like him?" you argue.

The agent gestures to the other side of the freeway. "Take your pick," he says. "Except for that one with the sideburns. And that one on the end. They're my clients, too."

You shout a few queries over to the other convicts, asking for some summaries of their life stories, hoping for a germ of something you can run with. But they're all the kind of killers and rapists that a reader would have a real problem sympathizing with. Nothing like Keith.

With your hopes dashed yet again, you leave the highway and vow never to go back.

"I wasn't meant to write a book," you conclude when you arrive at your desk the following Monday. "I was meant to sit at this desk and complete the tasks as outlined in my job description." You never attempt to write again. On your lunch break, you go to a clothing store and buy a few pairs of khaki Dockers.

THE END

Clean and Sober

Your first night in AA, when you walk into the gymnasium, more than half of the attendees greet you with their arms wide open, as if you were reuniting with your old high school buddies. It turns out that the meeting is composed almost entirely of people you partied with the night before you woke up next to Laura Kennedy. They're all thrilled to see you, because they feel they owe their recovery to meeting you. Every one of them went into AA after that night, deciding it was time to make some changes to avoid ending up like you.

Unfortunately, you don't recognize a single one of their faces.

"Hey!" one of them shouts. "I assumed you were dead after you fell through that skylight. Great to see ya!"

"I'm sorry I left you to deal with that bus driver on your own," another one apologizes sheepishly. "After you took off all your clothes and started running around the bus screaming 'Balls-Free Transportation Authority,' I had to hightail it out of there at the next stop because I already had a warrant out on me."

"Is that baby okay?" another one asks. "The one you delivered?"

Another attendee, a great bear of a man, all brawn and gray bristly cheek, approaches you slowly with his lips quivering. The room is silent as he steps close to you. You look up at him, and like a damn bursting, his mouth cracks open and a peal of sobs pours out.

"You got some kinda nerve showing your face in here," he says as he pulls you to his chest and holds you tight. "It's gonna take all the nerve you got, but keep coming back."

The others lean in to pat your back or join in the group hug. Even though you've no memory of ever having seen any of them before, you feel as if you've come home.

THE END

Get the Word Out

At Kinko's you sit down at one of their pay-per-hour computers that has a camera hooked up and you set about creating a poster. At the top in big letters it reads:

HAVE YOU SEEN ME?

Then you take a photo of yourself and insert it into the middle of the poster. Underneath you type:

DID I PISS YOU OFF LAST NIGHT?
WAS I THE GUY WHO:

Made a pass at your girlfriend/boyfriend?
Peed in front of/on you?
Took a swing at you?
Reached over your shoulder and stole a chicken wing off your plate just because I saw them and was hungry, and when you asked me what the fuck, I tried to kiss your face?
Threw up on you?/your friends?/your family?/your shoes?
Grabbed your boobs?/balls?
Ruined your game of video golf?

IF YOU RECALL ME DOING ANY OF THE ABOVE, OR ANYTHING EQUALLY REPREHENSIBLE LAST NIGHT, WANNA TELL ME OFF? THEN MEET ME AT THREE O'CLOCK TODAY IN THE UPSTAIRS SEATING AREA OF THE

BURGER KING ON 40TH ST AND 8TH AVENUE.
NO WEAPONS!

You print out the poster and take it up to the counter to ask for a hundred copies. The kid looks at the poster, then at you. Then he shrugs and takes it to a copier for printing.

It isn't long before the copier jams and the manager comes out of his office to fix it. He takes his sweet time, tugging several crinkled up posters from inside the guts of the copier. You watch his every move. It's going to take you hours to get all those posters hung around town and you want to strangle that manager for how much of your time he's wasting. Once all the jammed sheets are removed, he meanders to the other side of the production area to toss the ruined posters into the trash. Then, finally, he closes up the machine and presses the button to resume your print job.

Before returning to his office, the manager stops when he catches sight of you and your scornful look. His eyes move to the posters in the trash. Then he looks up at you again.

"You got a lotta nerve showing your face in here again, son," he says.

Uh-oh.

You tell the manager that you're in a hurry and if he wants to tell you off for whatever you did wrong last night, he should come to the meeting. But he doesn't say anything. He just bends down to a cabinet, again taking his sweet time, and he pulls out a bottle of Windex and some paper towels. Then he comes out from behind the counter and shoves the Windex and towels in your hands, and he drags you to a copier with an "Out of Order" sign on it. He lifts the cover on the screen and points to the brown skid mark on the glass that you apparently left behind last night after photocopying your damp anus. You spray the Windex and begin to scrub.

Back at the counter, you're given your copies and you pay. Before you're allowed to leave, the manager takes one poster off the top of the pile and tacks it to the bulletin board by the counter. You thank him for the use of his bulletin board space, and you head outside to start papering the city with your face.

If you want to pay the homeless to help you post your flyers,
PICK UP BOOK TWO AT A BOOKSTORE NEAR YOU!

If you just want to post them all yourself and get to the Burger
King, YOU'RE JUST GONNA HAVE TO WAIT. . . .